PREFACE

Aqua Monde Corporation Press Release

Close your eyes. Picture your ideal vacation. Perhaps, you find yourself lying on the crisp white sands of the Gulf of Mexico. Maybe, you are exploring the volcanic coastline of the Azores. You could be relaxing in the geothermal spas of Iceland, or listening to the waves crash from a serene Bure in Fiji. How about some high rolling excitement at a world-class casino, or the thrill of a theme park. The choices are limitless but imagine if you could enjoy all these adventures on one life-changing trip.

Open your eyes. You no longer have to dream. Aqua Monde is truly paradise on Earth. Located in the Mid-Atlantic, built on a foundation of volcanic islets, the engineering marvel of the 21st century is the only destination worthy of the most discerning traveler.

Our resort coastline comprises the finest imported Floridian sand. The Polynesian inlet features water-top huts built by traditional craftsmen from Tahiti. Geothermal spas combine mother nature's energy and the most advanced Nordic technology. The World's largest water park provides thrills for the whole family while adults can enjoy one of our three Diamond rated casinos. When you're relaxing you can rest easy knowing that your eco-friendly vacation is also helping to change the lives of millions of people.

Beyond the lavish accommodations, world-renowned scientists are hard at work. Aqua Monde's team of engineers are using cutting-edge technology to convert the ocean into clean water. Our desalination center uses a graphene electrolysis filtration system to provide drinking water to Saharan Africa. The sodium chloride by-product is shipped at no cost to meet the need for salt across West Africa.

We have also tapped vast reservoirs of crystal clear drinking water that has been locked beneath the ocean for millennia. AM crystal water is regarded as the best tasting mineral-rich water in the world.

In fact, it is the best water in history. Don't believe us? Then ask the archaeologists who found it. Believe it or not, this sprawling complex began as a dig site for archaeologists from the University of Florida. While searching for ancient artifacts, team leader Kevin Newman discovered the vast water reserves. The excavations for ancient remains yielded very little, but his work led to this far greater discovery.

As a socially conscious corporate entity, AM reinvests 20 percent of every vacation dollar spent, to bring free salt and clean water to Africa. As a guest here, you are changing lives one dream at a time.

DROUGHT

The sky over Monrovia was grey and hazy but despite the intense humidity it hadn't rained for days. Flomo Johnson made his way down the clanking gangplank connecting the vast cargo ship to the dilapidated dock. A disinterested National Port Authority officer glanced briefly at his passport before waving him onshore.

Freeport harbor was especially noisy this time of year as merchants maximized shipments ahead of the tempestuous summer months. Cranes rapidly unloaded containers laden with salt from Flomo's vessel as similar machines stacked all manner of rubber products in the hulls of the neighboring ships. Flying under a United States flag, the AM Inspiration was the largest and newest of the boats in the dock.

After an arduous eight hour voyage across the Eastern Atlantic, Flomo was preparing for a few days at home. He couldn't wait to strip off his vibrant green jumpsuit with the words Aqua and Monde emblazoned across the back. There was no escaping work though. Reminders of his employer were scattered all along the shore. Water tankers emblazoned with the company logo rumbled along the shoreline. Advertisements for AM Sea Salt were plastered across the bus terminal. Pamphlets for the firm's bottled water littered the streets.

With surprising agility for a man of 50, Flomo weaved his way across the crowded street. Traveling by cargo ship was far from glamorous but the next leg of his journey involved the even more modest confines of a 1983 F-series Ford truck. Originally painted white, it was now largely brown. It was difficult to distinguish the rust from mud but based on the engine sound alone, the vehicle was clearly on its last legs. The driver was Flomo's youngest cousin Enoch. A one-time medical student, he had dropped his studies when his parents fell on hard times. He had worked on the family farm for three years until it was no longer viable. He now made a meager living selling scrap metal out of his truck.

"Hello-o, how are you-o cousin?" Enoch excitedly asked. Flomo was always happy to see his young relative but he lacked the energy for a lengthy chat.

"Not bad-menh."

Enoch took the hint. He twisted the dial and the crackling radio came to life.

"Right-o, this is Star Radio with DJ Green and the boys bringing you the latest hits. But first, we've got to talk about these exploding seagulls. People are saying they are blowing up at Ce Ce Beach and sending ice particles everywhere. What kind of lunch have these birds been eating? " Enoch sniggered. Flomo gave him a disapproving look. He didn't feel like chatting and he certainly wasn't in the mood for a sensationalist radio broadcast.

"Right-o," said Enoch compliantly as he turned the dial off and consented to let Flomo ride in peace.

Technically, Liberia was home but it never quite felt like it to Flomo. Before the civil war, his prominent family ran an export business. Their wealth enabled him to enroll in boarding school in England. He eventually graduated from the London School of Economics before moving into the investment world. That seemed a long time ago now.

Flomo had left his job on the London Stock Exchange five years ago. He vowed to leave the corporate world behind him. Now he found himself working for the corporate icon of the 21st century. No one on the manmade island knew of his past career. Few would have guessed that someone who once had been among the top earners at one of the biggest investment banks in Europe would choose to enlist as a janitor in the middle of the Atlantic ocean. Flomo did not care much for money. He had seen his country destroyed by a war that was as much to do with greed, wealth and lack thereof as it was to do with politics. He did not need to work for money. He chose to work for the greater good.

As the sun began to sink toward the horizon, Flomo's painfully dull journey was approaching its end. The truck shook violently as it staggered over the poorly defined dirt road that led to his family's farm. A dip through a water-logged crevasse in the road splashed wet mud all over the windshield. Enoch steered his way past the corroded chicken wire and heaps of corrugated metal that served as an unofficial boundary line between the Johnson farm and the neighboring plots of parched earth. His father, Jefferson was standing by the ramshackle hut that the family had called home in recent years. Enoch turned off the engine and Flomo clambered out of the filthy vehicle.

Typically, guests there would cause a commotion among the free wandering chickens the family farmed but this time there were none to be found. "We should be able to fit a lot in here," Flomo said referring to the truck. His uncle nodded and silently led him past the house. The old man was in his seventies and did not look as if he would make it into his eighties. The last few strands of hair on his head fluttered wildly in the light wind. He had a filthy blanket wrapped around his skeletal torso and wore the same frayed pair of Levi's Flomo had bought him from London some twenty years before.

Jefferson stopped a few yards past the house and stretched a bony finger out towards a mound thirty or forty feet away that emitted a fetid smell. The ground around it was cracked and dry. The only color, in the drab locale, was provided by the gargantuan lime green pipes that ran through the field and into the distance. The color scheme matched Flomo's overalls. As did the words emblazoned on them "Aqua Monde Corp."

His uncle was keen for Flomo to explore the putrid mound but Flomo realized that to go any closer he would have to go alone. He took a handkerchief from his pocket and tightly pressed it against his mouth and nose. With his free hand, he tried to swat away the increasingly thick swarm of flies that blocked his route. He leant down to try and avoid the majority of the insects and took a close look at the mass of rotting flesh he had come to see. There were three carcasses of shorthorn cattle that were so emaciated he could barely recognize them as the animals he had helped rear. Stacked upon the dead cattle were the remains of a dozen chickens and two scrawny lambs whose thin layer of wool had been sheared before their deaths. Life had never been easy in this part of the world but there had always been sufficient water to keep the animals alive. That was until Aqua Monde was built.

Spiritual locals claimed the water deity Mami Wata had caused the drought to show her displeasure at mankind. She ruled the waters and didn't welcome the intrusion of a manmade monstrosity in the heart of the Atlantic. Flomo knew the cause of the water shortage was the island but he also knew the reasons were based in science rather than superstition.

He had seen enough for now. The somber spectacle of devastated livestock only served to strengthen his resolve. He hurriedly backed away from the mass of rotten flesh. "Uncle," he said "N'mind ya. Mami Wata will be avenged. I will take them. I will take them all. The cattle, the birds . . . they will send their own message. They will have their own revenge." Jefferson stared intently at Flomo. "Don't let us down," he said "we have suffered too many times. Don't let them win again. Mami Wata is waiting."

ODYSSEY

"There she is luv," said Billy Bradshaw as he grinned excitedly "our holiday is right there across the sea. Beautiful ain't she?" The 'she' that he referred to was Aqua Monde, or as it was more commonly known 'the eighth wonder of the world.' It had taken twelve years and an estimated one trillion dollars to build. It was the largest manmade structure on Earth, built around a small gathering of volcanic rocks some five hundred miles north of Ascension Island and a similar distance from North West Africa.

The man-made island was divided into four sections; a resort, a power plant, a desalination complex, and a scientific research center. The money men who bankrolled its existence boasted that it used only renewable sources of energy and it was hailed as the blueprint for 21st-century living.

Billy Bradshaw was an unlikely candidate to be among its first visitors. He was a dustman from East London who had benefited from an insurance payout after the untimely death of his older brother. Billy took the bulk of his newfound wealth and spent it on tickets for himself, his eight-year son Ben, and his girlfriend Sam to travel on a luxury liner to the island. He could have bought a functioning car or paid off his mortgage but six weeks of oceanic adventure surrounded by the rich and famous was too much for him to pass up. Billy had never been abroad before, a fact that would not be altered by this 5,000 mile round trip to an island that technically was not another country.

"Oh yeah, lovely Billy. Are you gonna rub this cream into my blisters or what?" snapped Sam angrily. She wasn't used to hot weather. She had naively exposed herself to three hours of direct sunlight on the top deck sunbeds during the first day of the cruise. She spent day two in an ice-cold bath, days three and four moaning in agony, and the rest of the trip itching and peeling. Like Billy, she was the wrong side of forty although a lack of hygiene and maintenance particularly around their teeth and hair meant that they both looked at least a decade older. Thirty-year smoking habits had also taken their toll on the duo. Although each claimed to be no more than "social smokers" the overflowing ashtrays in their cabin told a different story.

Billy knew he was out of place on the luxury yacht but reveled in the attention he received for the black socks, raggedy sandals, brown shorts and union jack vest he wore each day. His son Ben was a spiky-haired, freckle-faced mischief-maker who spent most of his time ogling the bikini-clad female passengers. Billy reluctantly took the bottle of aloe vera from Sam's hand and gestured for her to lie on the sun-chair nearest to them so he could apply her cream.

Ben, never one to waste a chance to misbehave, decided to unravel a rope attaching a lifebelt to the door. The lifebelt fell onto the deck. Ben deployed it as a makeshift soccer ball. The Bradshaws thought they were alone but they were being spied upon by pairs of eyes from the suite on the second tier.

Paul Jackson was not only the wealthiest man on the boat, he was also the owner. A Yale graduate, Wall Street whizz kid, hedge fund founder, and multi-billionaire. Despite his credentials, he was barely known outside Manhattan. He was tall, dark and more handsome than he would have been before the advent of plastic surgery. He was a decade older than Billy but looked a similar number of years younger than the Englishman. His teeth would not look out of place alongside keys on a Bosendorfer grand. The only smoking he had ever done involved the finest cigars Cuba had to offer.

In the deck with him was his long-term employee Jim Boyle -- a Floridian of Scottish and Italian descent. Short and fuller in build than Jackson, he did share his love of the tanning bed and gold wrist-wear. Boyle had successfully run two of Jackson's favorite British golf courses before landing his new role as Aqua Monde president. He did not like Jackson. In fact, he despised him, although the two were to most onlookers virtually identical personality types. Boyle had always done a wonderful job of disguising his true feelings.

"We sell tickets at $22,000 a pop and we end up with a boat full of rednecks!" Jackson said wistfully.
"Ah, I don't think they're rednecks Paul. Most of the people on board are British," said Boyle.
"Well, what do you call rednecks in Britain," asked Jackson.
Boyle shrugged his shoulders, "I don't know. Welsh people?!"
"Haha," roared Jackson "you're a funny man Boyle. An asshole but a funny man."
They each finished up their glass of scotch and stepped out onto the deck.

The second tier of the boat consisted of Jackson's penthouse suite, the captain's deck, one pool, two hot tubs and a helipad from where Jackson's chopper was now preparing to depart. The pilot gave the thumbs-up signal as Jackson handed his empty tumbler to Boyle. "See you on the other side," he said. He had meant on the other side of the watery expanse between the boat and the man-made island. His parting words would soon have a very different meeting in the mind of Boyle.

On board the helicopter was Jackson's 19-year-old Latvian fiancee as well as his personal photographer. The latter was there to take snaps of his airborne arrival at Aqua Monde that were supposed to adorn the brochures at the grand opening event the following week. Jackson climbed aboard the doorless flying machine and gave the pilot a firm pat on the back.

On the deck below Ben tossed the lifebelt over the side of the vessel and turned his eyes to the helicopter overhead. "Cor blimey, that things blowing my hair all over the shop," griped Sam from her facedown position on the sunbed. "Stop moaning you grumpy old bat," Billy retorted. Satisfied that his girlfriend's hair had resumed a stationary position, Billy set to work soothing her sores.

Ben picked up Sam's cell phone and started to film the grand departure of Jackson over the ocean. The scene reminded him of something he had seen in a James Bond film. "Cool," he muttered to himself. Onboard Jackson was feeling a little nervous.
"Hey George," he said over his headset to the pilot "look out for

those seagulls."

"Don't worry boss," said George, "They won't come too close." Jackson nodded in acceptance but the large flock of birds was hurtling towards them at an ever-increasing pace.

"George," he said "they are coming right at us. Take some evasive action can't you?"

It was already too late. Dozens of seagulls encircled the helicopter in midair. Jackson rose from his seat. Clasping the edge of the doorway for support he leant his head outside in amazement at the apparent recklessness of the birds. No more than a few feet above his head, one of the birds stopped flapping its wings and glided straight into the rotor blades. Its head went up; its feet down and it's midriff sent a fountain of blood and feathers into the air. Horrified, Jackson swung around and stood back up against the inside of the craft. George the pilot was furiously knocking on the windscreen trying to
scare away a particularly large bird that was resting with its wing spread and its belly blocking his view. "Move," George yelled, "move you stupid bloody thing." The bird lowered its head as if to address him. In an instant, a guttural force burst from the bird sending flesh in every direction. Its skeletal remains slid down the windscreen causing its spine to get entangled in the wiper.

On the boat, Ben was watching the whole scene unfold in stunned silence. One by one, the birds threw themselves into the path of the copter causing it to sway one way then the other. There was a rapidly forming slick of blood and sliced feathers accumulating on the ocean's surface. The water beneath the hovering craft gushed wildly due to the swirl of the rotor blades. As if responding to an unseen signal, the survivors of the flock suddenly dove into the battered rotor blades.

The copter went up five feet, then tilted to the left as the crew on board tried to fight off the vicious animals. Then with a crash that seemed to shake the whole ocean, the copter tipped onto his back and plummeted into the sea. The impact spewed shards of metal in every direction. It was too far away and the boat engine too noisy for the screams to be heard but Ben knew he had just seen four people killed. "Dad," he said as he finally lowered the cellphone to his side, "I want to go home." He turned teary-eyed to Billy who stood and cast his eyes onto the blood and debris filled sea.

ASSIGNMENT

Padraig Coyle could feel his heart pounding. It was the same internal drum that had echoed against his mattress all night long. Today was the day he feared he would lose his job. He knew he should be thinking of positive things to say in his defense but the only words formulating in his mind were the expletives. He longed to unleash his fury against the powers-that-be from the Knox Media Conglomerate. Seven years covering local politics in West Florida had worn him down. The promise of an international correspondent posting was now a faded dream.

Padraig had begun his career on the London Gazette in his native England. He followed his best friend and renowned photographer Danny Hill to Tampa to work for the locally owned Enquirer. Two buyouts later, he was working for the second largest media firm in the world. He had experience, his co-workers were fresh-faced rookies. The last long-term employees were his boss -- who had been let go yesterday -- and Danny, who had been told his future lay elsewhere. Now it was Padraig's turn for a one-on-one showdown with the all-powerful Florida executive Claudia Navarre.

Padraig impatiently glanced at the clock on the wall. By his reckoning, it was five minutes slow. That fact, coupled with his obsessive habit of always being early meant that he had already been waiting for what seemed like an age.

He tried to look composed but his right leg seemed to have a life of its own. Every few minutes he became aware of its incessant bouncing on the terrazine floor of the waiting room. It was something that seemed to irk the new secretary who kept peering down her nose at him every time his jitters reached a crescendo. Each time she caught his eye, Padraig gave a half smile and a raised eyebrow by way of apology. Every time she looked back at her monitor he changed his smile to a snarl.

He did not like her. He did not like any of the new employees. All the women were a blur of bronze tans, blonde hair, and tight fitting power suits. The men were clone-like Ken dolls with pedicured nails, dark hair and gold-plated cufflinks. Padraig looked out of place with his wrinkly white shirt, frayed tie, and ill-fitting khakis. He had the same hairstyle with a poorly defined middle parting that he had adopted at the age of 13. Half a decade of avoiding sun exposure meant he retained the pale, gaunt look that had been all the rage when he left England years before. Florida was never his cup of tea. The tepid UK job market drove him there. A continual lack of worthwhile alternatives had caused him to stay.

The secretary peered up at him again. Padraig out of habit started to apologize for tapping his foot until he realized that this time he had not actually done so. "You can go in now Mr. Coyle," she said. "Oh. Thank you," he meekly replied. Nobody had ever called him Mr. Coyle before. It unnerved him slightly. Such formality was usually reserved for court cases and funerals. It wasn't a good sign. He took a deep breath hoping it would lower his heart rate. It was to no avail. He felt as though someone was trying to punch their way out of his chest as he turned the handle of the frosted glass door and stepped into the editor's office.

Sitting in place of his recently departed boss was Claudia Navarre. She was a petite, Latina woman in her forties. "Take a seat, Padraig," she said gesturing to the empty chairs on the near side of the desk. She neither stood nor offered a handshake. This further rattled Padraig. "Thank you," he said as he anxiously took a seat. Her coldness, the company culture, all of it pointed to one thing: his termination. He was undecided as to which insults he should direct towards her when she made his firing official.

"Padraig," Claudia said as she leaned across the desk. "You're viewed as a valuable member of KMC and I want you to know that you have a long-term future here." Padraig was speechless. He had tried to anticipate everything she might have said to him but this was most unexpected.
"Valuable?" he asked, seeking reassurance.
"You don't think that's a credible view of you?" Claudia asked.
"Oh yes, I mean of course. Just nice to hear it once in a while you

know?" he responded.
Suddenly he was no longer aware of the blood flowing through his veins at high speed and his breathing began to normalize.

"The thing is Padraig," Claudia continued "that there are going to be some changes around here. Mick retired as editor and we're replacing him with Ashley."
"Ashley? Isn't she the one who was a Miller Lite girl?" asked a stunned Padraig.
"I believe her background was in marketing. Yes," said Claudia.
"Anyway, we're going to be taking things in a different direction."
"What direction is that? A lad's mag?" Padraig sniped. His fear of dismissal had been replaced with a sense of bitterness. He felt that the old hacks were being replaced with what he saw as gormless "bimbos" He could not see a place for himself working alongside or underneath them.
"Look, Padraig," Claudia said "I like you. I get you. You are English but to people who don't know you most, of the time you come across as serious or hostile. Our clients want..."
"Our clients?" interjected Padraig, "I'm sorry I didn't know we had 'clients' I thought we were a newspaper. I thought we went around digging up dirt on sleaze bags and grilling politicians!"
"We're not a newspaper," said Claudia "We're part of a media conglomerate and it is in our interests . . . financially… to conduct ourselves in a way that isn't going to be viewed as negative or hostile."
Padraig could not think of a verbal response so instead rolled his eyes and followed it up with a smirk.
"Padraig," Claudia said "You're old school. I get it, but our owner wants to help push a certain political agenda. You aren't someone best suited to that."
"So I am being fired?" he asked.
"No not at all. You're going to be an international correspondent."

Padraig's emotional rollercoaster was on the move again. He had been waiting seven years to hear those words. A broad smile burst across his usually stern looking face.
"I'm glad you're pleased," said Claudia "and some other good news. As you know we're cutting all our photographers and going to

freelancers. But, we're going to make an exception and send your old pal Danny with you. We'll need a good photographer where you're going. So for the next 3 months or so, he still has a job."
"Where am I going?" Padraig asked.

Claudia paused for a second. She anticipated a negative response. The delay caused his smile to evolve into a grimace. Finally, Claudia blurted out "Aqua Monde."
"Aqua Monde? Is that some kind of bloody joke?" demanded Padraig.
"No," Claudia retorted, "its grand opening is coming up. It is going to be a big event. Lots of celebs. It should be fun."
"Fun?" Padraig exclaimed, "If I wanted fun I could go and write a review of Busch Gardens for you."
"Look, it will be a good experience for you and when you're done who knows? Maybe we can send you to Moscow or something, and you can write about breadlines and Mafiosa" said Claudia.
"Anyway, it is not all that dull. There was something going on with exploding seagulls down in that area. If you're bored check that out." With that final comment, she gestured towards the door and then turned away to make a phone call. Padraig had expected many things from this meeting but Aqua Monde and exploding seagulls were not on his agenda.

MONROVIA

"I'm in Liberia," said Padraig "no Colonel Gaddafi was Libyan. .... Liberia. ...it is a country. Remember that Leonardo Dicaprio film about diamonds...it was Sierra Leone but it is next door...I can't think of anything Liberia's famous for. ...No, it's not in Eastern Europe it's in West Africa... No, it's not near the pyramids... look I've got to go Nan. Bye." He clicked off his cellphone and sat down on the hotel bed.

The Memba hotel was currently the only place in the neighborhood with functioning electricity. That fact hadn't escaped the notice of local residents who were queuing up for access at the extortionately priced internet terminals on the ground floor. It was a decent hotel by international standards but positively otherworldly by comparison with other local offerings. The Memba was the place to meet foreign businessmen and wealthy nationals on business in the city.

The room Padraig was staying in was the least expensive. More comparable with accommodation found at the grottier hotels nearby. It comprised twin beds, a 16-inch black and white TV, and a view of a dark alley. Crucially, the meager dwelling offset the cost of flying to the remote location. Unbeknown to Padraig's roommate Danny, the duo were supposed to be in Rio. Unbeknown to their boss who was funding the Rio stopover, they were in Liberia.

The African nation was technically nearer to their final destination. However, there were no direct US flights. They flew via Charlotte, New York, and Accra to reach the West African nation over the course of 40 hours travel time. A direct flight to Rio would have saved them $2,000 and at least 30 hours. The reason for the extra travel was Padraig's uncontrollable curiosity.

He had been reluctant to take up his assignment in Aqua Monde until he Googled the manmade isle and found a series of website postings involving ill-fated seagulls of the kind Claudia had mentioned. One video in particular had caught his eye. It was purportedly filmed on a cellphone by a student on the Monrovian shoreline. He was recording footage for his sociology class of young children scavenging for scrap metal on the beach when a commotion could be heard behind him. As he turned, a crowd of people ran past the cameraman until he finally got a clear shot of three seagulls passing overhead. As they came directly over his path, one by one they seemed to swell up and explode causing mayhem on the street below. The poster on Youtube stated that similar sightings had been occurring for the past week. On each occasion, small fragments of ice were found in the vicinity of the ill-fated birds. It was as if, he wrote, 'that the ice caused them to burst.'

Padraig knew that neither his editor nor his photographer would regard this as anything more than a fraud. After hours of reading posting after posting about similar things occurring as far away as St. Helena, Angola and Uruguay, he was curious enough to investigate. The consensus among those making the reports was that the birds had come from or passed through Aqua Monde. There was no tangible evidence to back these claims. Nevertheless, after taking a cursory glance at a globe, Padraig quickly realized that if nothing else the island was at the epicenter of the alleged activity.

Among the problems now facing Padraig was the fact that having come to Monrovia he had absolutely no idea where to find any of the people who saw the birds explode. He had a roommate who may not react kindly to the news he'd been duped into coming there. He also had a time constraint as it was a mere 24 hours before their ship departed for the island.

He was trying to think of a way to explain the situation when Danny suddenly burst into the room clutching a 12 pack of Club Beer. He looked tired and unhappy. "This place is a hell hole. This crap is the only beer they sell and it cost me $40 dollars for a 12 pack," he moaned as he tossed the beer bottles onto Padraig's bed. Danny was shorter and rounder than Padraig. Years before he had been the skinny athlete at school. Once he entered the working world, an unhealthy diet and lack of exercise had led to a rapid weight gain. He had shoulder length dirty blonde hair. A badly kept beard covered most of his face. He wore a leather jacket to try and maintain a tough guy image that had never really existed beyond the confines of his own mind. He also has a tendency to overdose on musky aftershave. The stifling humidity, and lack of air-conditioning amplified the unpleasant fragrance to unholy levels.

"I emailed Claudia," Deacon continued much to Padraig's dismay.
"What did you email her about?" asked Padraig fearing his deception had been exposed.
"I just said Liberia isn't fit for us to visit," replied Danny.
Padraig was mortified, "You idiot?"
"What is your problem?" asked Danny.
"Claudia doesn't know we're here," Padraig hurriedly explained, "she thinks we're in Rio."
"Rio?" Danny retorted.
 "Yes. We were meant to go there but I wanted to find out about these exploding seagulls that have something to do with Aqua Monde. I booked the flights here which cost a tonne more and saved a few quid to balance the books by sharing a room and hitching a free ride on the water tankers. Claudia never would have known until you blew it."
"Wait a minute," Danny said, "you lied to me too. How is it my fault that you lied to everyone?"
Before Padraig could respond his cellphone came to life with a shrill ring. The caller ID lit up with the name 'Claudia.'
"Crikey," Padraig said, "what am I going to say?"
Danny found himself in the role of an unwitting accomplice "I don't know!"
Padraig pressed talk. "Hi, Claudia how are you?'
The voice on the other end demanded to be put on speaker.
"OK boss you're on speaker now so we can both hear you."
"Now please tell me why Danny sent me an email about Liberia?" she asked sternly.
"Ohhh," said Padraig "he's been emailing everyone. We watched this show on TV about Liberia. It really interested him so he's been contacting everyone about it." As the words left his mouth Padraig wanted to sink into a hole in the ground. Danny grimaced at him.
"Is that true Danny?" Claudia asked.
"Yes, it was on PBS," Danny mumbled. Padraig mouthed "PBS?" back at him as the two men realized that an alibi about watching a

US TV station was hardly plausible if they were supposed to be in Brazil.

"PBS?" snapped Claudia.

"Yes," said Padraig meekly "well the Brazilian version…it's called … BBS."

"Never heard of it."

"It's really good we're watching it now actually," Padraig was gaining confidence "there's a documentary about … coffee … and soccer." His confidence disappeared as he realized how cliched his lies were.

"Coffee and soccer?" asked Claudia scornfully "what kind of combination is that?"

Padraig ventured a response "it's called . . . 'Things Brazilians like.'" He winced as the words left his lips. Danny pounded his head against the wall in animated frustration.

"OK, whatever. Fine. Well since you guys are in Brazil I need you to do me a favor?"

"A favor," asked Padraig fearing she'd ask for some kind of unique Rio souvenir.

"Yes. Todd from accounting has to do an audit on our South American journal so he's heading there tonight. He's never been there before so I told him you'd show him around. Is that OK with you?"

"No," replied Padraig.

"What do you mean 'No'?"

"I don't want to?" Padraig replied

"Why?" demanded Claudia.

"He's boring," quipped Padraig.

There was an awkward pause before Claudia revealed, "Here is here with me."

"Don't tell him what I said," said Padraig who was half inclined to hang up the phone and jump out the nearest window.

"We're on speakerphone," said Claudia.

"Oh . . . Hi Todd. How are you?" said Danny sheepishly as Padraig buried his face in his shirt.

"I'm fine," replied an irritated male voice.

"Look we're going to have to go Claudia, there is a Carnivale procession headed our way and the costumes are causing static on the line," at this point Padraig had given up on trying to sound credible.

"Carnivale doesn't take place this time of year," said a bemused Claudia.

"They started it early this year," said Padraig.

"Because of the recession," chimed in Danny. Padraig punched him on the arm.

"How would that help in a recession?" demanded their boss.

"They want to have it . . . Before people run out of money?!" Padraig's response ended as a question.

"Have you two been drinking?"

Padraig held the phone to his mouth, gnashed his teeth together and blasted a flurry of saliva through them to mimic white noise. After a few seconds, he mumbled "you're breaking up" and switched off the phone. He turned to Danny "Do you think she bought it?" he asked hopefully.

"Do you think she's on crack?" said Danny.

"Well screw her anyway she's probably going to fire us when we're done. I hate even answering to these mid-level management nobodies. Did I tell you I did my family tree on Ancestry?" asked Padraig.

"What did you find? Long lost ancestor who left you billions?" quipped Danny.

"No." snapped Padraig "Royalty? I am a direct descendant of Henry II."

"So you're descended from a King," scoffed Danny "and yet here you are holed up in a dilapidated roach motel. Where did it all go wrong for your family?"

Padraig shook his head wistfully. "Generational decline my friend. Generational decline. But we had a good inning. Three hundred years we ran the show. Puts little upstarts like the Roosevelt's and Bush's into their place as but a speck of dust in history."

Danny was unimpressed. "I read a while back that 49 of the US Presidents were descended from King John. So it seems like we are all from the same origins."

"King John?" mocked Padraig, "That black-sheep of the family couldn't keep his pants on. Plus he was three hundred years before Henry. By the time you get to the start of my tree, the ancestry line is very exclusive."

Padraig was prepared to deliver a lengthy explanation of his genealogy but Danny had questions about other concerns. "So why did you have us come to Liberia anyway?"

Forgetting his noble roots for a second, Padraig suddenly became energized.

"Well I told you there have been alleged sightings of exploding seagulls here," he said. "A bunch of people think they have something to do with Aqua Monde so I figured we could check this place out en route. The alternative was a trip to Ivory Coast, where similar things have occurred but I have been there before so it was also an excuse to travel somewhere new. Granted, from a tourist perspective Liberia isn't the Ivory Coast."

"You mean Côte d'Ivoire," Danny replied.

"No, I mean Ivory Coast. Why do people keep calling it Cote d'Ivoire now anyway on the footie?" Padraig asked.

"Because that's its name."

"No," snapped Padraig "that is its French name. We don't call other countries by their French name like France for example. We just call it France, not le Français," said Padraig. "Well if we did it would be like calling it The France which sounds stupid," Danny replied.

Padraig's racing mind had now moved off onto another tangent. "We call Ukraine the Ukraine though," he said. "That's kind of weird when you think about it. I mean I could see calling Iceland the Ice land because it is the land of ice as it were but why is Ukraine 'the' Ukraine?"

"Maybe," suggested Danny, "it's to distinguish it so we know that it's not just any old Ukraine but it is the definite article."

"You know there is only one Ukraine right?" Padraig remembered that neither geography nor etymology were of much interest to Danny.

Snapping back to the situation in hand he mustered a weak but sincere apology. "Sorry about not telling you what my plan was. I just figured you wouldn't want to come."

"Well," said Danny "fortunately for you I did some Googling of my own so this may not be a wasted trip."

"You read about the seagulls?" asked Padraig expectantly.

"No," snapped Danny firmly, "well yes, but that isn't what intrigued me. I did some research on Aqua Monde. The corporation behind it, and who is pulling the strings."

Padraig was surprised at the photographers' journalistic investigating "You been reading the Wall Street Journal and the Financial Times?"

"No" Danny scoffed "Wikipedia."

"The ever-reliable reader-sourced website," laughed Padraig "Did you make sure to check Yahoo Answers too?"

Danny was unimpressed. "The page on Aqua Monde had credible sources, Reuters, the UN. Legitimate stuff."

"So what did you learn?" Padraig asked as he sensed there was something intriguing to be revealed. "Well," Danny said "the head honcho Paul Jackson. He made his billions operating some scumbag hedge fund. They made a mint after the last recession by purchasing delinquent third world debt. Municipal bonds from Harare, Kinshasa and national debts. They caused a stir when they won a court case against the nation of Malawi. An international tribunal upheld their right to collect the debt. With interest and penalties, the debt amounted to $4 billion. That's equal to 80 percent of Malawi's Gross Domestic Product."

Padraig was appalled. "So they bankrupted the country?"

"No," Danny responded. "They would have, but a protest petition went viral attracting the support of humanitarians including Bob Geldof, Bono, and Pope Francis. The Hedge fund decided to write off the debt. Overnight, the CEO Paul Jackson had a Scrooge-like metamorphosis. He entered into this trade deal with the country of Liberia whereby he would supply the country with free drinking water and salt, in return for simply waving shipping charges and tax duties. They constructed a five hundred mile pipeline to bring desalinated water from Aqua Monde to Monrovia. The desalination leftovers like salt and bicarbonate soda are shipped there and distributed by government-backed charities."

"There has to be some financial gain in it for him?" queried Padraig, "are they putting African salt suppliers out of business? kill the competition then cut the free supply?"

"Seemingly not" replied Danny. "I guess China is the world's major salt supplier followed by the US. There is a legitimate need for salt in Africa, and their legally binding contract has a duration of 200 years."

Padraig gnawed off a few centimeters from his left thumbnail as he excitedly digested the details of Danny's discovery. If this Jackson really was a reformed Scrooge McDuck then he could produce a quality article during his trip to Aqua Monde. If this was all some dastardly ruse to screw over Liberia, then he could be the investigative journalist to bring it to light. Either way, he had more to write about than the kind of fashion-oriented guff his boss was expecting.
"I like it," Padraig said "Good work Danny. As soon as we have checked out these seagulls we can get to work on learning a little more about this benevolent billionaire."

It had been a long day. Padraig and Danny had prowled the shoreline of Monrovia looking for evidence that the online stories and videos they had seen were anything more than an elaborate hoax. Their search had yielded no results.

The beach was virtually empty as the sun began to set across the Atlantic skyline. It was a beautiful scene but most of the locals had more mundane affairs to occupy their mind than the colors and tones of the atmosphere at dusk. Danny had taken the opportunity to take hundreds of snaps of the capital just on the off-chance he could sell them at a later date to the Associated Press. Padraig had nothing to show for his efforts other than slight heartburn. Both a food connoisseur and penny pincher, he had snacked all day on Fufu -- a local pancake-like delicacy available from street vendors. Washing it down with ginger beer had done little to resolve his heartburn.

"So the nearest we got to 'exploding seagulls'" Padraig said, "was that war vet who offered to strap a grenade to a bird." Danny sniggered.
"On the other hand," Padraig continued "It would appear that the whole shoreline is a giant advertisement for Aqua Monde."
It was no exaggeration. Everything from bottled water to potato chips seemed to carry the logo of the corporate entity. Even the sachet of antacid powder Padraig had picked up, was produced with bicarbonate soda courtesy of Aqua Monde.
The two Englishmen meandered from the beach on to the firmer ground at the mouth of the St Paul's river.

"We had better head to the ship soon. The port is about a 20-minute walk due East from here" said Padraig.
He had made arrangements for them to travel by boat to Aqua Monde. The vessel in question was the AM tanker Intrepid. The Corporation which owned the boat had been given a contract by a UN-sponsored charity to help re-establish the city's water supply. This involved restoring the decaying White Plains water treatment plant in the city. The full restoration would take several years. In the

interim, a transatlantic pipeline of desalinated water was fed into eight circular holding tanks at White Plains. From here, tankers transported water around the city. Ultimately, the plan was to have a clean energy and water sanitation plant here that would be the blueprint for similar ones all built by AM corp. across West Africa.

The White Sands plant was perched on the river bank directly in front of Padraig and Danny. Thus far it had failed to capture their attention. That was about to change. The quiet evening scene was abruptly disturbed by the sound of sirens as four police cars came flying down the street towards the journalists. The vehicles skidded to a halt outside the water plant. Two heavily armed policemen jumped out of each car.
"Who are you?" one of the police officers demanded of Padraig.
"We're journalists," he said, "what is going on?"
"Rebels. A rebel attack" replied the officer. Satisfied that the Englishmen were not the rebels, he turned away from them and followed his colleagues through the main gate and into the plant. Danny pulled his camera from his jacket pocket and followed the men. Padraig hesitated for a second before noticing the sign at the plant's entrance. "Property of Aqua Monde Corporation," it read. His mind started to race: the exploding seagulls, the hedge fund billionaire, police hunting terrorists. Everything seemed to be inexplicably linked to Aqua Monde. Chasing armed police officers was not something Padraig had done before but he uncharacteristically decided to throw caution to the wind in search of a story. Behind the main gate were two small pools containing brackish water. Beyond those lay acres of interwoven metal piping which fed vast blue tanks at the far end of the complex.

The police officers were gathering around one vast pool of water at the epicenter of the complex. Danny started taking snaps as he headed their way before his own eyes had even had time to focus. Padraig finally caught up with him as he reached the edge of the walkway. The police officer who had briefly interrogated them stretched his arm across the two men's chests as if he feared they might fall in. The pool was a ghastly scene. The water was bright red and full of lumps of congealed blood. Rotting carcasses of cattle floated silently on the surface. The stench was foul.

"Who did this?" asked Padraig of the policeman.
"Rebels," he replied.
"I thought the rebels were done. The war's over?" Padraig responded.
"In boxing, the bell rings for the round to end sometimes but the fight isn't over," said the officer
"Perhaps it is time for round two. Who else would poison the city water but rebels? Enemies of the people?"

Padraig nodded in agreement before giving the officer's statement some more consideration. The 'rebels' presumably wanted to gain control of the city. Long-term they would need the support of the residents. Poisoning the water supply was not likely to endear the city's population to the combatants. Attacking a water supply was more like something a foreign army might have done -- in medieval times. The intent being to harm the people not to liberate them.

Danny, satisfied with his haul of bloodied carcass photos, started taking pictures of the policemen. An angry glare and a raised nightstick convinced him that it was probably time for him and Padraig to leave the scene.
"Let's get out of here," Danny suggested.
"Yeah," said Padraig "probably best."

"I totally hate Kevin." No one disagreed with Anne Hyeron's statement. Kevin Newman had made himself universally unpopular among scientists, archaeologists, and anti-capitalists when he decided to go and work for Aqua Monde. He was the scientist who had discovered vast amounts of mineral water trapped in volcanic rock in the middle of the ocean. It was his further investigation that had led to the uncovering of the ancient remnants of a lost civilization. In the absence of a more official name, the mysterious people were being referred to by the media as the Atlanteans.

Turning his back on his own scientific scruples, Kevin quit his job at the University of Florida and went to work for Aqua Monde. He was well compensated for making the career change. Moreover, with the title of Scientific Advisor, he could still claim to have some academic leanings. While his erstwhile colleagues lobbied the UN to preserve and protect the volcanic outcrop, Kevin decided to cash in. He spoke out in favor of the commercial exploitation of the mineral water reserves. Making cash off valuable water supplies was a surefire way to make enemies in an increasingly drought-stricken world. But Kevin's descent into notoriety didn't end there. Archaeologists from every corner of the globe were queueing up to examine the prehistoric remains on the islands. Kevin deliberately downplayed the significance of his own discovery as he knew archaeological research could delay the extraction of the water. AM was paying his wages, and the sooner the work began, the quicker he could fill his bank account. Corporate lobbyists supplemented Kevin's dubious recommendations by making generous donations to weak politicians. Within months, AM Corp had secured exclusive rights to turn the unique locale into a giant money-spinning operation.

Despite Kevin's best efforts, UNESCO did make a slight concession to the cultural world. A small team of archaeologists would have access to the ancient sites albeit for a brief period of time. Ironically, Kevin's alma mater the University of Florida was selected as the institution to oversee the work. Kevin's one time protege Anne, was now the leader of the group. She and her companions had just two months to finish their work before Aqua Monde demolished the ancient remains to make way for the world's largest domed swimming pool. Anne, the broad-shouldered, ruddy-faced, self-proclaimed "tomboy," had enjoyed the company of seemingly less superficial and learned folk like Kevin. She had never imagined that one day he'd replace his toupee with an implanted flat top, and ditch his tweed for leather, but he had and she was decidedly bitter about it.

"We need to find something to screw him up," Anne said "something so unique that the UN heritage foundation will say it has to be preserved."
"How about his one piece, red striped bathing suit that he wore all summer," joked Terrance.
"They would probably demand that thing being destroyed" Anne chuckled "for the inhumanity of him wearing it."
The duo both laughed out loud as they recalled the odd site of the 60-year old professor taking water samples on the coastline in an oversized Edwardian bathing suit.

Terrance, like Anne, was a postgraduate student from the University of Florida. He was an African American from East Gainesville, the same city where the University was housed. His closest friends had dreamt of playing football for the college. Terrance and his twin brother Leroy had been keen scientists since they both got microscopes for Christmas at the age of eight. Leroy was fulfilling his dream of working at NASA while Terrance was much further from home sitting aboard a converted Oil Tanker called the SS Nimrod on its way from Monrovia to Aqua Monde.

The research contingent was completed by a Scotsman of Chinese descent, Kenny Tsang.
Like the others, Kenny was in his mid-twenties but was smaller and less athletic looking than his colleagues. Kenny was sleeping in the squalid cabin the trio had been assigned having spent most of the preceding 3 days driving their dilapidated UN jeep from Bamako to Monrovia. Anne and Terrance had a habit of treating Kenny like the junior member of the gang. He was always the one who had to load and unload the equipment and clean up the mess when their experiments got out of control. For the most part, he didn't mind, as

the diminutive Scotsman was easily the most laid-back and cheerful of the three.

"Who are they?" Terrance asked Anne. She looked towards the far end of the ship where two unfamiliar men were in discussion with one of the Nigerian crew members.
"I don't know," she said, "maybe more corporate bods?"
"Not being funny but they hardly look corporate." Even from a distance, Terrance felt that Danny's scraggly facial hair and ponytail would look out of place in any white collar workplace.
"Maybe they're journalists," Anne suggested.
"No way. reporters these days are high maintenance. They aren't going to get down and dirty in Liberia."
"Yeah true. Probably crew members."

Terrance turned away satisfied with their theory. Anne was curious about the duo. The taller man seemed fidgety. He was gnawing away at the stubby fingernails on his left hand while twiddling the hair above his ear with his right hand. He was glancing around nervously taking mental note of anything and everything. He looked out of place, uncomfortable and yet totally absorbed with the scene around him. The scruffy man seemed perfectly at ease talking to the machine-gun carrying Nigerian crew member about whatever it was that they were discussing. He was focused on the chat while his wide-eyed colleague seemed anxious to explore the deck.

"Hi there." An unfamiliar voice finally broke Anne's watch of the newcomers. She turned around to see an African man in his fifties with an outstretched hand awaiting reciprocation. Terrance shook the man's hand first.
"Hi. I'm Terrance and this is Anne."
"My name is Flomo. I am with the maintenance crew."
"Nice to meet you, dude. That doesn't sound like a Nigerian accent" inquired Terrance.
"You're astute," laughed Flomo "for an American. I am from Liberia but for my sins, I picked up a hint of the Queen's English. I was in the UK for a long while."
"Who are those guys," Flomo asked with a glance in Padraig and Danny's direction.

"We thought they might be with you," said Anne "maintenance guys? Crew?"

"No," Flomo replied, "they aren't crew. I saw them talking to the police onshore about 20 minutes ago."

"Maybe they're FBI," Anne suggested excitedly.

"Maybe," said Flomo. "If they are, I wonder if they are here to investigate for AM corp. or to investigate AM corp."

"If it's the latter I am onboard," Anne said proudly.

"Me too, young lady. Me too." Flomo wore the stock issue uniform but he wasn't here to work.

"How's that?" asked Terrance. "I mean, we are archaeologists so we have our beef with them because of the cultural damage they're doing. But you work for them. You're Liberian. I thought everyone out here loves them. Aren't they solving the African water crisis and all that?"

Like any good scientist, Terrance sought the truth through asking the pertinent questions. There was something about the Liberian that made him uneasy. He seemed remarkably well spoken for someone who was ostensibly there to mop the deck.

Flomo turned to look at Terrance. He tucked his lower lip under his incisors as he carefully contemplated his next words.

"You know where the name Liberia comes from right?" he asked Terrance.

"I mean, it was a freed slave colony wasn't it?" offered Terrance " so I guess it is derived from Liberty."

Flomo nodded in affirmation. "There are lots of people fighting for Liberty even today, Mr. Terrance," Flomo said. "Some of them get dressed up in camouflage and balaclavas, shoot off guns. Others . . . well they just play along with the bad guys. Watch, study, observe. Wait for their moment to use their brains." Flomo prodded Terrance firmly on the forehead with an outstretched index finger.

"Keep your friends close Mr. Terrance," Flomo said as he glanced at Anne, "but always keep your enemies closer."

Anne caught Terrance's eye. She was intrigued to learn more about this chatty janitor. Terrance was less impressed. He responded to her excited look with a roll of his eyes and a slow shake of the head. He had determined that Flomo was a 'player.' Giving off this air of mystery to impress Anne. Terrance wasn't so easily swayed.

Padraig and Danny finished their conversation and marched briskly over to the watching trio. Padraig awkwardly extended a handshake in their general direction. No one was quite sure who the handshake was intended for so his hand hung in the air for an uncomfortable length of time. Padraig was an introvert. This bungled attempt at connecting had required him to step outside his confining shell. In the awkward silence that followed he withdrew it in a huff. "Forget it," he murmured.
"Excuse me?" snapped Anne "what was that?"
Padraig looked away "come on Danny let's find some people to talk to who aren't rude."
"Rude?" exclaimed Anne. "You guys barge into our conversation unannounced shove a hand in our faces and then get all pissy because none of us has the gumption to be the first to shake it and introduce ourselves."
"Who the hell are you anyway?" demanded Terrance.
"I'm sorry," said Padraig "I got off on the wrong foot. I get nervous. I am just sort of grumpy because I'm tired."
"Or cause you're an ass," countered Terrance.

Anne could see the embarrassment on Padraig's face. She knew many academics who were not blessed with social skills. Perhaps Padraig deserved a second chance.
"Let's start over shall we," Anne said." Everyone take a deep breath. This is Flomo, our new friend from maintenance, the wise guy is Terrance and I am Anne. We're with the scientific group. Now, who are you two? "
"I am Danny and my uncouth friend is Padraig. We're journalists."
"British? You're MI6," responded Flomo.
"Excuse me? "said Padraig.
"MI6 agents always say they are journalists as their cover," Flomo explained
"So what do journalists say they are?" asked Anne
"MI6," Flomo replied. "Probably here at the behest of the Hedge fund who donated millions of pounds to the Conservative party that won the last election and lobbied the UN to give this man-made island international status. You guys are worried about the insurgents right?"

"No. You're completely wrong," said Padraig "but you seem to be very well informed for a maintenance man."

"He is" mocked Terrance "he is here to spread liberty."

"I wasn't always a maintenance man," Flomo revealed, "I had a very good career in the city of London but I came back to my country after the war to help clean up the crap."

"So you decided to grab a mop and clean up the literal crap rather than the metaphoric kind?" asked Padraig.

"Somebody has to," replied Flomo sadly.

"So how does Liberia benefit from you working at Aqua Monde?" asked Padraig.

Flomo was silent; he realized he had already said far too much. He had intended to keep his counsel private but his gregarious nature had already undermined his plan.

"Don't answer that yet," said Padraig "but luckily for you, I am a hack, not a spy. An entertainment reporter no less! But, that's just my official role. Personally, I am more interested in finding out why people poison water supplies and things like that."

"I don't want to add to the janitor's conspiracy theories," quipped Terrance "but if you're an entertainment journalist, why aren't you flying in with the celebs? The maintenance crew boat isn't exactly a great place to find out who is wearing Versace for the grand opening."

"Like I said," Padraig snapped "I have my job to do but I also have my own interests. Nobody said I couldn't do some investigative freelancing on the side."

AQUA MONDE

The foghorn let out three loud blasts as the first official group of visitors marched down the gangplank onto the world's newest island. Billy Bradshaw and his family led the sheepish travelers ashore. Behind him was Mike Patel, an Indian businessman who'd made his fortune owning a chain of gas stations in Texas. Patel and his wife Gita had come on the trip to mark his retirement. Thus far, he wished he had stayed at work. Patel had heard about the trip from a long time neighbor and now travel companion Hugh Pompidou. He was an active 80-year old water buffalo farmer. He'd spent most of the trip discussing water sanitation with Paul and Barbara Laws, a middle-aged duo of semi-retired Geography teachers from Essex in England. The three of them silently followed the procession off the boat.

No one had thought much about the leisure aspect of the trip since they witnessed the horrific helicopter crash 48 hours earlier. To reassure the new arrivals of their safety, the Vice President of Entertainment Cathy Furman had invited Security Chief Robert Beauchamp to be among the welcoming committee. The weary passengers were directed towards an oceanside amphitheater for their formal welcome. On stage at the front of the open-air site were Furman, Beauchamp and a specially arranged New Orleans jazz band. The surprisingly melancholy draw of the trombone somewhat reflected the mood of the watching audience. The musicians finished their routine as the last attendees took their seats.

The mock Greek amphitheater sat in front of the 'Futurescape' hotel -- a mirrored monstrosity towering over the rendezvous point. All the doors and windows were decked out with reflective glass. Primarily, it helped maintain a temperate atmosphere inside but it also added a layer of privacy for the guests. As with all the hotels, every guest room featured a thermal jacuzzi powered by the simmering lava beneath the island. The appliances were voice controlled. Bedroom doors could be opened with iris scans though magnetic cards were provided for traditionalists. Three outdoor pools with a variety of water slides separated the hotel from the garish looking casinos. Pink neon signs adorned the gambling dens to provide an authentic 'Vegas' feel. The new arrivals were keen to get to their rooms but the inevitable formalities had to come first.

"Welcome friends. My name is Cathy Furman. I am the Vice President of Entertainment and my job is to see that you have a good time." She winked seductively as the last words left her mouth. The audience was unmoved.
"Vice President," yelled Mike Patel from the back "where the bloody hell is the
President?"
Furman had been hoping for a warmer reception. Blonde haired, skinny, and with an inflated opinion of her own good looks she had hoped by batting her eyelids she could quickly cause the passengers to forget the horror they had witnessed. Realizing their mood she stepped back and nudged Beauchamp forward.

He hadn't done much public speaking in the 30 years since he left the army. His experience prior to that was limited to barking instructions at new recruits. An Englishman and veteran of the Korean action, he was now the no-nonsense face of Aqua Monde's 'world-class' Security operation.

"Ladies and gentleman," Beauchamp cleared his throat before continuing "what happened the other day was a tragic accident but rest assured we will be taking precautions to make sure it doesn't happen again."
"Precautions," cried Patel, "what will you do sir? Jail all of the sea-birds?"
The rest of the audience laughed and applauded whilst an embarrassed Beauchamp retreated back to the rear of the stage. Furman decided it was time to abort.
"If you exit through the rear," she said, "our helpful staff will show you to your rooms."

With that, the welcome was over. Billy Bradshaw wearily rose from his front-row seat and exchanged head shakes with Patel. "Ain't exactly Pontins is it?" said Bradshaw "At least there you get a bleeding balloon for the kids."

"I didn't want a balloon." groaned his son Ben.
"Shut it Ben." snapped Billy's girlfriend Sam.
Patel decided against engaging the trio in further conversation and made his way toward the exit.

On stage Furman gave a steely-eyed stare to Beauchamp "you realize now," she said, "that if anything…anything else goes wrong that we're both screwed."
"What can possibly go wrong young lady?" replied the army veteran "this place is as safe as houses." Before Furman could answer, her cell started vibrating. She pulled it from her skirt pocket and read the message she had been dreading. "Boyle wants to see us … now"

Jim Boyle sat at one end of a large oak desk tapping his fingers rapidly upon a stack of papers that were scattered about in front of him. The boardroom they were in was on the top floor of the Futurescape hotel. Every side of the room had glass walls allowing a 360-degree view of the glistening ocean. To Boyle's right sat Furman and Beauchamp. To his left were his scientific advisor Kevin Newman as well as chief investment officer Owen Gaunt.

"We've got problems," said Boyle to end the lengthy silence. "Paul was killed as you all know. Our sympathies go to his family. Our job goes on though so we have to forget about him and move on." None of those present were close to Paul Jackson but nevertheless, they all twitched with unease at Boyle's coldness.

"New York doesn't want the media making a big deal about this. We need to have our grand opening and then after the dust has settled it will be time for the obituaries.
Beauchamp, you need to make sure no one has any footage on their cell phones or camcorders that can get out on Youtube and kill our share price."
Beauchamp wasn't sure what was being asked of him "How am I to prevent that? I am sure someone on the boat got some snaps."
Boyle leant across the desk menacingly "You're the security guy figure it out! It's what we pay you for. Make up some excuse if you have to but search rooms, delete memory cards and help the five of us keep our jobs."
Beauchamp nodded his agreement.
Boyle continued, "What did we find with regard to the crash?"
Beauchamp sat up straight and answered "some fingers, one male torso, two severed heads…" He was mid-sentence when Boyle slammed the desk in frustration.
"I don't want to hear the forensic details, you idiot. I want to know if we have a cause!"
"My apologies sir but beyond the birds we have nothing," Beauchamp replied.
Owen Gaunt looked sheepishly across at Beauchamp and asked "the torso … was it Jackson?"
"Affirmative," replied Beauchamp.

Owen shook his head wistfully "I figured. I saw him fall out of the copter and it looked like the rotor blades took off his head. On the next go round, they caught him right in the lower groin. Ouch. Poor man."

"Are you done?" asked Boyle furiously. Gaunt nodded.

"So Gaunt, how much did you get in new investment commitments from the boat passengers?" Boyle was expecting a figure in the millions but he was to be disappointed.

"Well Jim," said Gaunt "I am working on a couple of pretty good prospects. Mike Patel is a gas station owner. Kind of a tough bargainer. He wants me to waive my commissions in order to invest."

"What did you tell him?" asked Boyle.

"I told him to take a hike and come back when he is ready to get serious."

"Find him and tell you'll waive your commissions," commanded Boyle.

"I am on one hundred percent commission Jim!," Gaunt protested.

"And you've made no sales after being at sea for a week with a bunch of wealthy people with nothing better to do than spend money. Waive your fees this time otherwise you'll be 100 percent unemployed." Boyle wasn't in the mood for excuses.

"Prince Faisal, our largest non-corporate investor will be flying here for the opening ceremonies in place of Paul. Cathy, you make sure his every comfort is taken care of. Gaunt, you make sure he plows some more cash into this venture. Beauchamp, you make sure he leaves here safely without a hair on his head out of place. Any Questions?" There were none. "No questions? Good."

"Jim," said Newman "I was going to let you know that the desalination plant is down again so we're waiting on engineering to take a look but it will probably be 48 hours."

"We are supposed to be shipping that water to Africa Newman!" roared Boyle.

"With respect, I did say the plant wasn't likely to be ready as soon as New York wanted."

Boyle glared at Newman, "Tell me we have made some progress with the extraction of the mineral water we are touting all over the world?"

"Sadly not," Kevin replied meekly. "After the first batch we tapped, we haven't been able to extract any more. It is inexplicable given the prevailing warmth of the volcanic rock but the aquifers keep freezing. Rock hard. We used drill heads to try and break the ice up but the drill heads keep breaking. We have access to water but we are struggling to convert it from solid to liquid form."

Boyle was perplexed and livid in equal measure.
"OK leave," he roared "All of you get to work. Go. NOW!" The four beleaguered attendees quickly exited via the rear doors.
Boyle was a man under pressure. Aqua Monde Corp. had made many bold promises and only its status as an independent 'island' prevented the truth of its failings from having already reached the media. The desalination plant wasn't producing enough water to keep itself running much less the fresh water it was contracted to send to West Africa.
The spring water that had been found in the volcanic rocks was being marketed as the 'most mineral rich and purest water in the world,'. It wasn't ready for mass bottling yet. The underground aquifers were inexplicably freezing. Meanwhile, most of the crew at the springs plant had been sequestered to help at the desalination plant. Far from aiding Africa with fresh water, the whole island was currently being kept open with water secretly smuggled in from that parched continent.
24 hours from now, the world would be watching and Boyle would either be a hero of Wall Street or suddenly unemployable.

Clank! Clank! Clank! Metal being thrust against metal was the unpleasant sound that served as Padraig and Danny's unwelcome early morning alarm call. Danny woke momentarily then rolled back over and resumed his sleep. Padraig was too frustrated to think of ignoring this latest disturbance. After a night disrupted by his roommates snoring and the numerous sounds emanating from the ship's nearby engine room, he was wide awake. Even without the noise, he'd have struggled to get a good night's sleep in the catacomb-like cubby holes that passed for bunks on the tanker.

The small metallic room was pitch black without even a porthole for decoration. Padraig slowly palmed his way along the wall until he found the switch that activated the dim bulb hanging from a simple cord on the ceiling. Another impatient burst of door banging startled him as he scooped his dirty T-shirt off the floor. He quickly threw on the shirt and briefly wondered if the relative cleanliness of his khaki shorts would draw attention to the ketchup stains on his top. He pondered how his roommate was able to sleep through the door being battered. Having learned to sleep through his own snoring, Danny was immune to most things.

Padraig rubbed his crusty eyes clean, wiped his oily face on his bed sheet and unlatched the oval-shaped door. As it swung open he was surprised to see the smiling face of Anne with a huge wrench in one hand and a bottle of fresh orange juice in the other. "I was wondering if I banged the door loud enough to wake you!" Padraig felt that her remark didn't warrant a response.

She looked as lively as Padraig felt lifeless. Her blonde hair was neatly tied in a French plait whilst his was in disarray. "What happened to your hair," asked Anne, "you look like you've joined 'Flock of Seagulls'" Padraig wasn't amused.
"It looks like crap because I just woke up after finally getting about 15 minutes of sleep all night. Anyway, now that you're here how about some bacon and eggs or something? I'm famished!"
"I've got a protein bar," Anne said.
"I'm sure I can drop a line over the side of the boat and find something more appetizing than that. An old boot perhaps?" Padraig

was feeling grumpy.
Anne decided not to respond to Padraig's negative quips. "Well, we won't have to because we are about to dock. Oh, and what's up with Danny? Is he going to sleep all day."
Danny suddenly sat up "What time is it?"
"Time you made an appointment at the snoring Doctor," snapped Padraig. Danny flopped his head back onto his pillow as Padraig followed Anne outside.

She led the way up the narrow flight of stairs that connected their rooms with the main deck. As they exited, Padraig was surprised to see everyone else onboard ready to disembark. Terrance was guarding a stack of luggage at the gate that would open onto the gangplank when the anchor dropped. Beside him was a shorter Asian man, Kenny Tsang. The latter was engrossed in an application on his ipod and failed to notice the arrival of Anne and Padraig on deck. Terrance nodded by way of greeting at Padraig who responded with a smirk.
"Your hair looks like that guy from 'Flock of Seagulls," joked Terrance.
"The old ones are the best," replied Padraig with a menacing glare.
"Ignore him Terrance. He didn't get his beauty sleep," said Anne.
"I can see that," Terrance replied. Kenny finished what he was reading and suddenly acknowledged the new arrivals. He smiled at Anne and then turned to Padraig.
"Wow. You're here man!" Kenny laughed. Padraig licked his right forefingers and then slowly tried to paste down his wayward hair with the saliva. "How's that? Better?" No one responded.

"So what do you think Mr. FBI or MI6 man? Here it is. Aqua Monde," announced Anne.
Padraig looked over the side of the boat. Before him sat the vast structure of the Aqua Monde desalination plant. The main building looked like a huge aircraft carrier covered almost entirely in solar panels. There were dozens of containers surrounding it linked by a complex network of color-coded pipes. The small containers were about the size of a compact car and the largest were bigger than an average size house. Groups of men wearing green overalls and goggles were clustered in small groups taking readings from gauges

on the containers. The whole operation covered an area the size of a dozen football fields. Beyond it, in the distance, Padraig could seem the glass high rise that housed the executives who controlled the island.

"So is this where you work?" Padraig asked.
"No," said Kenny "we work over there." He pointed to the far right of the desalination plant that was directly in front of them. Padraig moved to the side of the boat to get a better view of what he was talking about. Where the desalination plant ended, a giant concrete wall began and stretched into the distance for what looked like miles. It towered over the ocean obscuring the view of the archaeologists' workplace.
"Behind that wall?" asked Padraig.
"Yes," said Anne "The original bits of land that preceded this monstrosity are back there. Since most of it was below sea level they drained it and built that wall to keep out the ocean."
Padraig was impressed at the size of the structure if not its appearance.
"It's fantastic," he said. "No, what is fantastic," retorted Anne, "is the archeological site they want to bulldoze to build more hangers and monstrosities. As if we don't have enough of that anyway. Now the corporations are turning the middle of the ocean into a concrete jungle!"

A huge thud rocked the ship as the boat finally docked.
"I had better make sure Danny is up." Padraig scurried away and down the staircase back towards his cabin. He was about to walk back into his room when he saw Flomo further down the hallway gesturing to him. Curious as to what the Liberian wanted he walked past his room and followed him through another oval shaped doorway into a large cargo deck. Inside were 4 containers similar to the ones he had seen onshore at the plant.

Flomo stood waiting by the tank at the back of the room. He waited for Padraig to catch up to him before addressing him. "Listen," said Flomo as he picked a wrench off the ground. He whacked it against the tank causing a dull thud. Padraig was bemused. "So?" He had no idea what the point of the demonstration was. Before Flomo could elaborate a group of mechanics came through and struck up a conversation with the African about the maintenance schedule. Padraig stood for a moment until Flomo jerked his head signaling for him to leave. Padraig did so, none the wiser as to Flomo's actions.

As Padraig stepped out of the room he saw Danny waiting for him with both their suitcases in the hallway. The two men made their way upstairs and followed the now exiting crew off the gangplank onto the dock. Padraig was surprised by the absence of any security officials or people of any kind at their arrival point. The group in front of him went through a set of glass doors that lead into a hallway. The hallway was connected to the warehouse-like structure that was the epicenter of the desalination plant.

Anne, Kenny, and Terrance were walking down a pathway that ran in front of the building towards a metal gateway. Beyond it rose a steel staircase that scaled the huge wall that encapsulated the archaeological site. Noticing that the journalists were trailing in their wake and looking totally bewildered, Anne instructed her cohorts to go on without her. Padraig had been hoping she would do so and called over to her, "So where are you off to now ?"
"Oh I thought I'd grab a couple of Pina Coladas, slip on my bathing suit and lay out by the pool," Anne replied.
"Sounds good to me," said Danny enthusiastically.
"She was joking," said Padraig "she likes to be sarcastic."
"That makes two of us then."
"Where are we supposed to go then?" Danny asked.
"Well if you're journalists ... as you claim, then there should be someone somewhere looking for you. If you're not journalists ... as I suspect, then you might as well snoop around until you get caught." Anne grinned cheekily, turned and ran after her colleagues.
"She's got a point," said Padraig.
"Let's get snooping," Danny smiled.

The obvious place to begin "snooping" was the huge building in front of them. Padraig was surprised at the apparent lack of security at the swinging glass doors that were the main entrance to the desalination plant. He hesitated at the entrance, half expecting to be apprehended by unseen guards. Danny was satisfied that they were alone and just pushed his way through the doors. Having taken one last glance over his shoulder Padraig decided to follow him.

They ventured inside the long glass corridor which led to another set of swing doors serving as the entrance to the actual building. The fact that the whole island was owned by a mega-corporation was reason enough for Padraig to want to dig for dirt. The seagull mystery together with Flomo's cryptic words only served to fuel his suspicions. The second set of glass doors were steamed up with condensation caused by the temperature difference from the hallway to the interior. Danny stretched his palm out in front of his colleague to stop him blundering through just as some workers passed by on the other side. Satisfied that the men had dispersed without noticing the intruders, Danny dropped his hand. Padraig cautiously pushed the door open. Inside were an array of tanks connected by vast pipes. No workers were to be found. Padraig gave Danny a thumbs up. The two quietly passed through the doors. The room was very similar to the ship they had been on. Very little color, lots of piping and white-washed metal walls.

"What are we looking for?" asked Danny who had quickly determined that they were unlikely to find much of intrigue in the plant.
"I don't know," said Padraig "that's why I am still looking." He briskly marched over to a truck-sized vat in the center of the room. There wasn't much to observe on it. After a few seconds glancing at it he turned away and absent-mindedly rapped it with his knuckles. The vat echoed with a loud hollow boom. Padraig swung around to face the vat again. He kicked it with the toes of his boot as hard as he could. The vat vibrated for a few seconds then went silent.
"Did you hear that?" Padraig said excitedly. Danny was unimpressed.
"The vats on the boat didn't echo because they were full," Padraig continued before kicking it again. Danny suddenly realized what he was getting at.
"But they're supposed to be bringing water off the island to Africa." Logic suggested the vats on the boat should have been empty while these should have been full with the next batch of water destined for Liberia.

"Exactly," said Padraig, "I think we've found the start of a fascinating piece of investigative journalism."

"Having fun gentlemen?" asked an unfamiliar voice from behind them. The journalists turned around and saw that they had been joined in the room by three new arrivals. At the front of the group was the lean, grey-haired and weary-looking Security Chief Beauchamp. Either side of him were machine-gun toting men wearing green overalls similar to those worn on the boat by Flomo and the maintenance crew.
"You know that we're on the high seas," Beauchamp said, "and stowaways are no more welcome here now than they were two hundred years ago."
Padraig smirked. "We're not stowaways, we're journalists."
"Journalists?" asked Beauchamp "the flight from Brazil hasn't come in yet and I didn't check you in from the cruise ship. I never forget a face."
"We came in on the tanker as …" Padraig decided he probably shouldn't implicate the crew members he'd paid for safe passage so left his sentence unfinished.
"Stowaways?" Beauchamp finished the sentence for him.
"Can you explain to us why these tanks are empty?" demanded Danny.
"The desalination plant has been having technical issues. The operations have been halted, not that it is any of your business gentlemen. Take them to security"

Danny looked at Padraig expecting him to explain away the situation. Padraig decided to stay silent. He felt that there may be more to be learned as prisoners than as guests. Realizing his colleagues' plan Danny rolled his eyes, sighed and then compliantly marched off behind the guards to security.

FOOLS GOLD

Owen Gaunt lounged back in his oversized leather armchair and bridged his hands across his mouth as he contemplated what he should say next. He sat just beneath his pride and joy — a stuffed moose head. He told his clients he slew the beast in Winnipeg. In reality, he bought it second hand at a flea market in Omaha. Across the oak table, which occupied most of his small undecorated office, sat Billy Bradshaw and his girlfriend Sam. The latter was analyzing the split ends of her bleached hair. The former sat on the edge of his seat waiting impatiently for the American financial advisor to speak. Gaunt's face was long and his heavily wrinkled brow gave him a stern look even when he was cheerful. His thick grey mustache reminded Billy of his Grandfather -- an uppity man from a harsher age who had intimidated him as a kid -- in much the way Gaunt was intimidating him now.

"Billy" Gaunt suddenly sprang to life "my father was a very wise man. He used to say to me 'son there is no point buying flashy things when you don't have a pot to piss in.' The question I have to ask you now Mr. Bradshaw is, whose pot are you going to piss in because I don't think you have your own."
Billy was flabbergasted. He had been expecting to get advice on investing. Instead, he was being ridiculed. Sam, who had been only half paying attention, suddenly processed the words that had left Gaunt's mouth and angrily slapped her hand on the desk.
"What are you trying to say he ain't got a pot to piss in Mr.? We ain't stuck up but we ain't doing too bad you know?"
"Perhaps I was too direct, but I did tell you when you came in that you'd have to excuse my candor if you wanted my advice."

Billy glared across the desk and firmly prodded Gaunt in the chest as he addressed him "I know plenty of blokes what pick up benefits without even bovering to get an honest day's work. I bust my behind out there keeping the streets clean making an honest living. I came in here ready to give you a fair crack of the whip. To see if you could give me some hot tips and you just shove it back in my face !"
"Mr. Bradshaw," said Gaunt calmly, "I am an investment advisor.

You live in government housing. You have no savings and you're on this trip because your brother bit the bullet ... God rest his soul. Investing isn't like betting on horses. I work by commission and if I work with people who have no money then I earn no money. So unless you have another relative ready to keel over then I would kindly ask you to leave."
"We don't have to sit around here and take this," said Sam.
"Exactly my sentiments" replied Gaunt.
"Rude" yelled Billy as he rose from his chair "that's what you are, rude! Bloody yanks you're all the same. No class!"
Gaunt was unmoved "have a great trip," he said mockingly as the enraged due stormed out of his office.

Gaunt had been a mediocre insurance and investment salesman for thirty years. The majority of sales he'd had were from elderly widows he bullied into products they neither wanted nor understood. Gaunt boasted that his approach was one of directness and honesty. In reality, he liked to be rude and to ruffle people's feathers, especially people like Billy Bradshaw who didn't know how to fight back.

Glancing at his fake Rolex he noticed that it was midday which meant that his next appointment was due. Right on cue, Mike Patel appeared in his doorway. Gaunt stood and extended a handshake as Patel made his way into the cozy office. "Your last clients left rather unhappily," said Patel as he reciprocated the outstretched hand with a firm shake. "I can pick my clients but I can't stop lunatics walking through my door," laughed Gaunt. Patel was surprised by Gaunt's remark and raised an eyebrow to signal his disdain. Gaunt realizing he had blundered, opened a small wooden chest on his desk and gestured for his guest to sample one of the Cuban cigars nestled inside. Patel again reacted with some disdain brushing away Gaunt's offer with a rapid hand movement.
Things were not going to plan for the investment broker. He decided to try and get down to business instead.

"Please take a seat." Patel nodded and sat in the seat Bradshaw had vacated. Another raised eyebrow from Patel prompted Gaunt to stop reclining in his chair and to sit bolt upright.

"Mr. Patel, or may I call you Mike?" asked Gaunt hesitantly.
"You can call me Mike."
"Mike you're a smart guy. You've run a business successfully. You've made a nice life for you and your family but doesn't there come a point when you want to kick back and enjoy yourself?" asked Gaunt. Patel thought for a moment then nodded his head in agreement.
"Now you know a good business opportunity when you see one right?" Patel again nodded in affirmation.
"If I had told you ten years ago that there was a company that had the technological capability to construct a huge island slap-bang in the middle of the Atlantic Ocean, you would have said I was mad! We're here Mike! Here it is. Now isn't that a company you want to invest in? Just think what they could come up with next." Gaunt had thrown his sales pitch on the table. He awaited his client's response. Patel stared at him intently and after a lengthy pause leant forward to give his reply.
"That's it is it?" he said "I just hand over my money to you now and then I will be rich. Is that how it works? What are you, Billy Mays? A thousand dollars per share or ten thousand dollars per bond and that's your sales pitch, Mr. Gaunt?"

Gaunt was perplexed. He had tried to approach the sales delicately on the boat but had been rebuffed. Now he had been direct and again had been knocked back. Yet the mere fact Patel had come to his office implied that he had some interest in investing.
"Mike," said Gaunt, "where did you learn the ropes on bartering?"
"I grew up in an Indian village and learned to trade at a very young age."
"An Indian village?" Gaunt was surprised "so you're an Indian?"
"Yes of course," said Patel, himself now perplexed.
"I thought you were one of those Pakistan Indians, not a Native American. Which tribe were you Apache? Cherokee? I have some ancestors who were Iroquois."
"I am not an American Indian Gaunt. I am an Indian."
"Forgive me I thought you just told me you grew up in an Indian trading village."
"We have villages in India too," snapped Patel.
"My sincere apologies. I didn't mean to insult your culture as a

Pakistan-Indian by confusing you with Native Americans. Not that doing so would be bad, as I am part Iroquois myself as I explained. So in a sense, you should take it as a compliment. Have you seen the film, Gandhi?"

"You have a highly unusual way of attracting new clients Mr. Gaunt," said Patel as he angrily rose from his seat.

"Well, I am sorry if I said something to upset you," Gaunt was genuinely bemused as to how he had caused offense.

"You have no understanding of sensitivity, geography, other cultures, business or sales, and I have to doubt whether you have any real knowledge of investments. Thank you, Mr. Gaunt and good day." Patel turned and left the office without a moment's hesitation. Gaunt sat deflated looking at his reflection in the glass-topped desk.

"I guess I am just getting jaded."

HIEROGLYPHICS

The archaeological dig site was a hive of activity. With only days until the grand opening of Aqua Monde, there were rumors that AM corp would want to speed up the construction on the site if the grand opening was a success. Any delays could mean valuable artifacts would be lost forever if time ran out before the bulldozers moved in. With limited time, the area being excavated was too large to enable a thorough investigation. The team led by Anne were concentrating on the areas that had yielded the best results early on.

A large canopy had been erected over a cave near to the edge of the site and within close proximity of the noisy water treatment plant. When the team from the U.S. had left for their shorebreak five days earlier, their support team had just started work on clearing soil and sand from the cave. They hoped to find evidence of deeper caverns they believed may hide more treasures. The excavation team had not been disappointed.

Henrik, a Swedish volunteer from UNESCO, had come to greet the returning scientists and led them excitedly to the canopied cave. He was over six feet tall, unnaturally thin with wispy blonde hair, small eyes, and a narrow, pointed nose.
"You won't believe what we have found here," he said as they neared the entrance.
"What is it?" asked Anne.
"There was a large rock blocking entry to further caverns. But it wasn't a natural occurrence. The rock had been chiseled to seal this entrance. We had to get the crane to lift it because it weighed probably eight hundred pounds and that is after taking the pneumatic drills to the edges because it was so perfectly fitted to the entrance."
Kenny stepped forward and peered into the dark hole at their feet.
"So the people here must have been pretty good masons," he said.
"The people here were much more sophisticated than we thought," replied Henrik.
Anne grabbed a flashlight from the heap of equipment piled under the canopy. "Let's check it out." Kenny grabbed two more flashlights, one for him and the other he handed to Terrance.

Terrance took it reluctantly.

"So what happened to just saying 'hi' then relaxing for a bit before work?" he said.

Anne and Kenny ignored his remark and took their first steps down the wooden ladder that was resting against the top of the cave. It was pitch black below and judging by the fact that the top of the ladder was about a foot from ground level, it was also going to be pretty far down. Anne went down first with Kenny carefully making sure to avoid her fingers as he followed. Henrik went next as Terrance hesitated before deciding to follow the group underground.

Anne had lost track of how many steps she had descended. Her flashlight was off and firmly clamped between her teeth. She stretched her foot out looking for the next rung of the ladder when she felt the familiar feeling of volcanic rock beneath her feet. She had reached the bottom. She yelled up to Kenny to let him know to be careful.

Anne clicked her light on as the others slowly reached the bottom of the ladder. She shone it directly on the wall in front of her and scoured the rock face looking for something as impressive as had been described by Henrik. Impatiently, she started pacing around until Henrik turned his own flashlight on and instinctively found the area of intrigue. He illuminated a rectangular doorway carved from the stone leading to a chamber that was directly behind the ladder they had just descended. Something could be seen glistening in the room.

Anne and Kenny excitedly ran through the door leaving the less than exuberant Terrance trailing in their wake. The giddy duo combined their flashlights' illuminating power to bring the back wall of the small chamber to life. The wall was covered in hieroglyphics that seemed to resemble those found in Egypt over 5,000 miles away. There were ten clearly defined rows of drawings. The upper levels showed pictures of people and animals. There seemed to be a flow of a story. Similar looking characters popped up throughout the pictures. The last row featured a tall light blue figure towering over what looked like buildings. Four consecutive sections showed the same picture of the white figure but in each one, the figure was taller and taller. The very last square of the display showed nothing but a chaotic whirlpool of blue and white color.

"What does it mean?" asked Kenny.

"Money," yelled Terrance from the back of the cavern. "Money for AM and money for us."

"I wouldn't count on it," said Anne "AM aren't exactly going to like this because whatever monetary value there may be in it there is much more cash to be made from developing this whole area into a resort."

"What's with the big blue guy?" asked Kenny.

"Some kind of deity," Henrik suggested, "Lots of ancient civilizations drew depictions of their gods in caves or their dwellings. Could be some kind of religious meaning. Perhaps it is recounting some myth."

"But why is he blue?" Kenny was puzzled by the drawings. His area of expertise was pottery so he was fairly new to parietal art.

"It could be tied to water," Anne chimed in. "The Egyptian god Nu was supposed to have been formed from water. He was often blue in artistic depictions. Lots of cultures had water gods. Poseidon for example. The Greeks did propagate the myth of Atlantis and we are in the middle of the Atlantic."

Terrance wasn't impressed with the Atlantis connection. "Atlantis is widely believed to have been Santorini," he commented. "Anyway, we are a long way from Greece. There are lots of legends of water deities in Africa. Nommos, Agwe, Mami Wata. If there is a cultural connection to be found I bet it is in West Africa."

"Wow," said Kenny who was genuinely in awe of his colleague's cultural knowledge "but I don't know if he is aquatic. Look at his shape compared to the other figures. He is very angular. Kind of like …"

"Ice!" Anne yelled excitedly.

Her supposition struck a chord with her colleagues. Their dig was being rushed in part because AM was trying to find more access points to tap the aquifers. The established access points led to nothing but rock solid ice.

"We should tell Kevin," suggested Kenny.

"Kevin?" Anne was enraged "Kevin would probably come down here and whitewash this whole wall himself if they promised him Disney tickets and a spa weekend for doing so. We can't trust that son of a bitch and I don't want anyone telling him or the rest of AM about it. Got it?"
Terrance shrugged while Kenny and Henrik agreed to her demands.
"We need to tell UNESCO," Anne said, "Henrik get on the phone to your people. This could be huge. A missing link to different cultures. The UN are the only ones who might give a damn about preserving this site."
"I wouldn't count on it," said Terrance "they are in AM's pocket."
"Then we tell the media," retorted Anne.
"There aren't exactly a lot of news crews around in the middle of the ocean," joked Kenny.
"No, but there will be," Anne continued "once the grand opening happens they'll be here from all over, and those two guys on the boat!"
"The spies?" asked Terrance.
"They said they were reporters so we brought them here and let them prove it."
"But what if they are spies?" asked Kenny.
"Then we'll steal their weaponized briefcases and hold them hostage until UNESCO agrees to save this site."

Anne was in no mood for negotiations of further delays. She knew that AM would happily bulldoze anything that stood in the way of their notion of progress. She had already seen how money had corrupted one archaeologist so she wanted to get this site publicized to the whole world before anyone else in her group had the chance to be bribed.

"Let's get out of here now before we draw undue attention to this site." Anne commanded "Kenny, seal it up. Henrik, try and get UNESCO on the phone. Terrance, you can find out what other media will be here and I will try and find those two from the boat."
"Yes ma'am," said Terrance mockingly.
"Don't piss me off," said Anne, "or I'll bury you down here."

She left the cave and scurried up the ladder. Kenny was amused that

Terrance's liking for her was unlikely to be reciprocated. He tapped Terrance on the shoulder and joked "give it up dude she's already in love with ancient man." Kenny made his way up the ladder behind her while the brooding Terrance stood unmoved. "Are you coming up?" asked Henrik. Without a word, Terrance slowly trudged his way up the ladder wondering what he could do to win Anne's attention.

Anne emerged at the surface anxious for her group to leave the dig site as quickly as they possibly could. She impatiently tapped her foot on the volcanic rock at the cave's entrance as her team slowly emerged. Terrance was the last to appear as he wearily drug himself out of the hole. "Right," said Anne forcefully "get to work" She spun around intending to head for the exit. To her astonishment, a crowd of people was gathered on the other side of the chain link fence that divided the dig site from the desalination plant.

"Who the heck are they?" asked Kenny, only half expecting a response.
Anne didn't know the answer but intended to find out. She briskly marched toward the barrier fence with the curious Henrik scuttling along behind her. Terrance was still brooding. He stayed with Kenny who was keen to avoid confrontation and hid under the canopy that housed the cave.
"What do you think you're doing?" yelled Anne as she finally came within earshot of the fence. The gate providing the only access point to the dig site swung open as she approached. A dozen people filtered through lead by a tall, dark-suited black woman. Anne stopped a few feet from her with Henrik peering over her shoulder. She looked scornfully at the woman whose name "Edith" was emblazoned across the lapel of her AM standard issue customer service uniform. Anne had encountered several of the female customer service representatives and felt that the criteria for hiring were based on having voluptuous figures -- as Edith had -- plus limited intelligence. The latter part of her assessment was incorrect although there seemed to be no evidence to contradict the former.

"Hello, my name is Edith." The customer service representative tried to disguise the anxious quiver in her voice brought on by the hostile reception. She took a deep breath before continuing. "Our VIP guests per their travel arrangements have unfiltered access to all parts of the resort prior to the official opening. The 'behind the scenes tour' was a major selling point of the trip." Edith gulped for air as she finished her explanation and waited nervously to see if it would placate the red-faced scientist.

"I don't know if you can read ... Edith," said Anne contemptuously "and judging by your blouse which looks two sizes too small, I imagine brains aren't your forte. This is an archaeological dig site and not part of the resort !" Edith was stunned at her rebuke. She felt a flutter pass through her stomach into her chest. Her temples pulsed and she felt as though she would lose control. Just as angry tears welled in her eyes she managed to take another deep breath and regain her composure.

"Please contact Cathy Furman if you have any questions." With that, she turned from Anne and walked over to rejoin her party. The group consisted of some of the people who had arrived by boat the day before. Billy Bradshaw was expectantly waiting at the head of the group for Edith to provide them with some interesting facts. As far as he could see she had brought them to a barren patch of land. Sam was disinterestedly coloring her nails green. Neither of them had noticed that Ben had remained outside and was attempting to scale a section of the fence.

"Ladies and gentlemen," said Edith, in her thick Southern African accent "this area is part of the small volcanic cluster of rocks that was the launching pad for the adjacent man-made wonder that we call Aqua Monde." Mike Patel and Hugh Pompidou had been surveying the area as both shared an interest in geology. The latter stepped forward to the front of the group eager to gather more information on the site.
"Excuse me miss," said the elderly man politely but feebly as he waved a bony finger in the air.'
"Yes sir Mr. Pompidou," replied Edith who was now smiling broadly as she regained her composure.
"I was just curious because outside the sign said 'archaeological dig' and I notice there is a tent across the way. I wondered what kind of

things they have found here."

"That is an excellent question," replied Edith. She paused unsure of how to follow up her first statement because she knew nothing of the archaeological finds and was loath to ask Anne.

"Well are you going to answer the bleeding question?" asked Billy impatiently.

"I'll answer" Anne marched toward the group menacingly. "There are untold treasures in there which could be irreparably damaged by a bunch of tourists breathing and sweating in close proximity to them. There has been an oversight here and we'll now have to ask you to leave."

"Hold on a minute we're VIPs" yelled Billy. He had no interest in excavations but felt an overriding desire to get his money's worth out of the trip.

"A condition of my package was unrestricted access," said Patel firmly.

Edith could sense that this was only going to escalate so decided to create an exit strategy. "Ladies and gentlemen we look forward to giving you a more thorough tour of this site but time has flown by already and we are expected in the refreshment lounge for morning tea. Please follow me." She confidently marched the group towards the gate from where they had come. As she brushed past Anne, she squinted her eyes and flicked her upper teeth with her lower lip as a gesture of disgust. She had retreated for now but she had unfinished business with the American.

"Get down you bleeding idiot," cried Billy as he finally caught sight of Ben who was dangling off the fence at least 10 feet above ground level.

"Alright I will," moaned Ben as he clambered down toward the ground.

"You can't go around acting like that or people will think we're not proper. Ain't that right," asked Billy of Patel.

Patel raised his eyebrows, sighed and nodded.

On the other side of the fence, Anne turned to Henrik. "Right no time to waste. We need to get cracking right away before Furman comes down here and sets up a Popsicle stand in our cave. Let's go."

Without hesitation, Henrik sprinted toward the gate. Anne turned towards Kenny and Terrance who had begun to meander their way towards her. "Snap snap!" she yelled. Time was of the essence.

Jim Boyle couldn't take his eyes off the unopened packet of cigarettes that was lying on his desk. He had been flipping in it from one hand to the other for five minutes until he dropped it on the last throw and it landed on his desk. He felt tightness in his chest and his heart was racing. One cigarette could ease his anxiety. He started to imagine he was taking a draw on a cigarette. He hadn't smoked in three weeks since his physician firmly told him to change his lifestyle or expect a heart attack. He had tried yoga for a day, running for two days and he was considering a course of acupuncture but the thought of the relaxing sensation a single cigarette could emit through his body was hard to resist.

Boyle was the boss but he was subject to the same non-smoking policy in place for all employees. He would have to resist his urge or risk one of his staff reporting him to headquarters. When he had started in the business world, smoking was widely tolerated. Cigars were the vice of choice among the successful. Tobacco had been omnipresent in the workplace until the nineties when health advocacy groups had driven smokers into the shadows. Boyle was only as politically correct as he absolutely had to be. He would like nothing more than to light a smoke, pour a scotch and give his incompetent staff a four-letter word roasting. Regretfully, he couldn't get away with doing any of those things in the modern workplace.

Frustrated by his lack of freedom he grabbed the packet of cigarettes and stuffed it into his inside jacket pocket. He needed a distraction so he shuffled his mouse to reanimate his computer monitor. A notification signal immediately popped up alerting him to three unread emails. He clicked the inbox to open the first. It was from Claudia Navarre of Know Media. "Who the hell is she?" Boyle mumbled under his breath as he opened the message and read its contents.

'My two reporters were supposed to fly to AM via Rio. No one at Rio airport has ever heard of them and I haven't had a communique from them in 48 hours. My boss is an AM shareholder so I need your

cooperation in locating them. These two are a pain in the ass so they could pop up unannounced. Attached are their photos.
Yours
Claudia Navarre
Know Media Senior Editor'

"So now I'm a babysitter for rogue journalists," Boyle said. He opened the attachment to see old passport pictures of Padraig and Danny. The black and white snaps were several years old but Boyle immediately recognized the duo as the 'stowaways' his hapless security team had apprehended earlier in the day. Boyle forwarded the message without comment onto his Security Chief Beauchamp. The next email populated his screen.
It was from his Vice-President of Entertainment, Cathy Furman.

'Jim,

That little bitch at the dig site just drove one of my new reps to tears. Kevin needs to find a new crew.'

Most of Boyle's senior staff had been complaining about Anne Hyeron and her archaeological crew for weeks. Kevin Newman insisted she was the best person for the job but her flare-ups were becoming all too frequent. Boyle didn't want any liabilities around when the grand opening got underway. He selected Newman's name from his email address book, attached the content of Furman's message and added his own comment.

'Kevin,

This has gone on long enough. Get rid of her. Now !'

There was one email left unread but this one's text was colored and a check mark signaled its urgency. It was from the Ministry of National Security in Liberia, an agency that through necessity was in close contact with Aqua Monde. The email was in the form of a special notice memorandum.

'Terror suspect.

A suspected terrorist named Flomo Johnson is sought by the Ministry of National Security in connection with an attempt to poison the drinking water supply in Monrovia.
The suspect was seen by eyewitnesses illegally gaining access to the city water treatment facility. He is believed to have used animal carcasses and waste products as the poisoning agent. The suspect is believed to be an employee of Aqua Monde and may have left the capital to travel to their remote facility in the Atlantic. He may be armed and dangerous. Attached are screenshots from CCTV footage at the water plant.'

Boyle scrolled down the page to view the six screenshots provided. A man in a green Aqua Monde uniform was standing beside a truck in the first. The other pictures showed the side profile of the man's head from close range as he was lifting a barrier to allow his truck access to the plant. Boyle was mortified. He had no idea who the man was but even the hint of a scandal involving one of his employees could send share prices tumbling. He quickly drafted a new email directed to Beauchamp, Furman and all security staff. He attached the Liberian's email and his own message 'Find this man now !'
He hit send and his screen returned to an empty inbox. "It doesn't rain … it pours," he said to himself as he pulled the packet of cigarettes out of his pocket.

CONTAMINATION

"You are free to leave gentlemen," said Beauchamp with an air of disappointment in his voice. He genuinely believed that he had apprehended two high-level corporate spies when he caught Danny and Padraig snooping around the desalination plant. He had been proven wrong by the email from his boss but his suspicions remained. Padraig and Danny for their part were more than happy to play the role of secret agents. They slowly rose from the thinly mattressed molded plastic bed they had been sitting on in the glass-walled 'interview room.' They had been spared the ignominy of being locked up in one of the steel encased 'detention cells.'

Beauchamp stared intently into the iris scanner located on the door. Nothing happened. Frustratedly he pulled his magnetic card from his pocket and slid it through the card reader. The glass door swung open. Padraig stepped forward and whispered into Beauchamp's ear. "Washington must have made the call," he sniggered. Beauchamp stepped back angrily.
"Don't think I won't be keeping an eye on you two," he said. Padraig smirked, turned and walked away.

Danny followed him silently as they made their way down the narrow hallway of the detention block until they arrived at the front desk. A life-sized animatronic Polar Bear stood by the exit as a symbolic warning to any would-be troublemakers. The bear let out a guttural growl as Padraig crept past.

As they approached the exit, the guard on check-in duty was laying back on his chair with his feet resting on the counter beside his computer monitor. Danny glanced down at the screen and was surprised to see a familiar face, Flomo Johnson.
"Padraig look it's the man from the boat."

The security guard suddenly aware of their presence dropped his feet to the floor and rose from his desk. He was very barely over five feet with short, tight, curls on his head and lightly tanned skin. He felt embarrassed that they found him lounging around but was also concerned that they had seen a classified security email.
"You know this man," he said, realizing he could use their accidental exposure to the email to his advantage.
"He was on our boat," replied Danny.
"The yacht?" asked the guard.
"We came in on your tanker," said Padraig "the one from Monrovia, with all empty tanks."
"Empty tanks ?" said the guard "well, of course they are empty. We kindly provide water to the Africans so the boats are always empty on their return."
"Always," said Padraig sarcastically.
The guard was bemused "Look I don't understand what you're on about but you say this man, this Flono, was on the boat ?"
"It's Flomo and yes he was on the boat. He was in the maintenance team," said Padraig.

Beauchamp had been listening to the conversation as he slowly walked down the corridor. "Thank you, gentlemen," he said "you may have helped us identify a dangerous terrorist but then, of course, you gentlemen probably already realize that. Am I wrong ?"
Danny and Padraig exchanged glances amused at the fact Beauchamp still believed them to be government agents.
"Never wrong Beauchamp, but what is wrong is the whole ambiance in your little dungeon area. Robotic Polar bears? That is very kitsch" said Padraig with a smile.
"Not purely robotic," explained Beauchamp "the hide, skull, and paws were attached to the frame by a very skilled taxidermist."
"Oh lovely," said Padraig sarcastically "even more tasteless than I had realized, Beauchamp."

Padraig had an idea. "Hold on a second. Beauchamp…Beauchamp," he began pacing around as if trying to remember something very important. "They didn't call you Bob Beauchamp, did they? Back in the day?" he said.

"Well yes, they did … or Bobby,"
"I think I may have read your files. Exemplary officer," Padraig continued.
"Read my files," said Beauchamp excitedly.
"May have," Padraig corrected him "you know I can't confirm or deny anything of a classified nature."
"Of course not," said Beauchamp who was now completely taken in by the ruse.
"So Bob," said Padraig "tell me what the deal is with this man."
"Sir we can't share this info," interjected the security guard but Beauchamp waved him away.
"These men are more important to our security than we are ourselves, young man."
Beauchamp shook his head and his dejected report sat back in his seat.

"The man on the screen, agent Padraig, is believed to be a Liberian terrorist of some sort. The government assured us the civil war truce was intact but of late there have been several instances of tampering with the water supply that we believe are the work of elements left from the war. You know that during the war the whole water supply of the city was disabled. These attacks bear the hallmarks of the rebels known modus operandi."

Padraig and Danny were thoroughly unconvinced. They had spoken to Flomo on the boat. While he had struck them as mysterious, he didn't seem like the kind of individual who would commit mass terror. Neither man though wanted to lose Beauchamp's trust.
"He's a menace," said Danny.
"Indeed," affirmed Beauchamp.
"We'll try to find him. He may trust us because he spoke to us a little," said Padraig.
"He may go after you for that very reason," argued Beauchamp.
"He may," said Padraig "but promise me this. If you catch him first, let us know. Let us interrogate him. We have methods …methods most people don't have. We can get him to talk. Do we understand each other?"
The security guard was shocked at the inference in Padraig's words but before he could speak Beauchamp planted a hand firmly on his

shoulder and answered for them.

"When we're talking about protecting citizens of my country," said Beauchamp "we do so by any means necessary. Of course gentlemen. You have my word."

Padraig smiled. This deception would be easier than he had thought.

Edith slammed her bedroom door behind her and threw her jacket onto the bed. She had endured a miserable day. Leading a group of disagreeable tourists around a resort like a ghost town wasn't much fun. The encounter with Anne and the subsequent debrief with HR and Furman had been even more draining than the incident itself. She was ready to relax. She kicked off her shoes, slipped off her skirt and headed into the bathroom that occupied about a third of the living space she was provided as a resident employee.

The bedrooms for staff came in two sizes: regular and deluxe. Anyone more senior than a manager got a deluxe room while the rest of the crew occupied 500 square foot studios. All of the rooms had an aquatic theme of some sort. Edith's room was in the 'pole zone.' This entitled her to a twin mattress mounted on a faux fur block, designed to look like a walrus -- with plastic horns and wire whiskers. Her bedside lamp was an Emperor penguin with a light bulb hidden on the underside of his beak. The wall was decorated with protruding wings of seabirds that were half plastic, half painted mural. The intent was to create an optical illusion whereby you couldn't tell from a distance where the painting ended and the protrusion began. It was an artistic concept that didn't translate well to her tiny cabin.

Some employees had views of the ocean. Edith's room had no windows. Instead, it had a huge painting of 'a whaling ship in Antarctica,' occupying the space a window would otherwise have filled.

She took off her shirt and tossed it onto the bed then walked into the bathroom. Everything in the bathroom was stainless steel or mirrored. She hated it as it made her feel self-conscious. She turned the steel knob that powered the shower and dropped her undergarments on the floor, casually kicking them towards the bedroom door. Stepping into the shower, she pulled the sea-life patterned curtain around, laid back and shut her eyes as the warm water began to wash the remnants of the day away.

The job had seemed a lot easier on paper. She stumbled across an ad at the recruiting center in Johannesburg University where she had been studying finance. Her original plan was to move back home to Windhoek and try to get a teaching job at the University of Namibia. However, her academic dreams were shelved when she was lured to Aqua Monde by the chance to work for a multinational corporation.

The training had been intense. The pay and benefits were better than most of the jobs her postgraduate friends were likely to get at home. At 23 years of age and having never left the southern part of Africa before, she was feeling homesick. The difficult to handle guests and co-workers were only reinforcing her sense of loneliness. The two places she felt at peace were in the shower with her eyes shut, and at night in bed because she could imagine she was anywhere.

The water felt different today as it cascaded down her forehead, onto her cheeks then over her shoulders. It felt harder like the alkaline heavy water in Johannesburg. She tried to massage the shampoo into her hair as normal but the water was now starting to splutter. The flow was not steady and it deteriorated into a stop-start staccato. Edith sighed, feeling that it was in keeping with the rest of her day.

She opened her eyes and shut off the water supply before restarting it in the hope that it would help the flow. It took a second for the liquid droplets to clear from her eyes. As she fluttered her eyelashes, a red bleariness remained. Her eyes were stinging slightly. She pulled the curtain back and stepped out to get a towel from the nearby rack. She buried her face into the towel. She then swept the lower part of the towel over her face and onto the top of her head to dry off her still soapy hair.

Her bathrobe as was typical was laying in a heap on the floor close to her feet. As she bent down to get it, she noticed what looked like a trickle of blood running down her right leg. A heavy but small looking globule slid past her knee then rapidly past her ankle onto the white tiled floor. She felt her face and looked at the mirrored wall for an undetected abrasion but the heat from the shower had steamed up the stainless steel.

"That's strange," she muttered, wondering how she could have cut herself as she put on the thick toweled robe. She walked over to the actual mirror which was directly opposite the shower. She stretched out her right hand to clear away the steamy layer of condensation that obstructed her view. As she cleared the mirror, she saw something odd behind her. The still running shower water looked dark, almost black. She spun around. A numb sensation rushed across her face from one ear to the other as she saw the shower head pumping out nothing but thick, congealed, crimson-colored droplets of blood.

Edith let out a loud scream then ran from the bathroom into the bedroom. The thought of having bathed in blood caused her to squirm. She looked at the tops and bottoms of her feet, the palms of her hand and her legs for signs of remaining blood. To her horror, her whole body was speckled with tiny crimson droplets as if she had been to a poorly operating tanning salon. She couldn't wash off in the shower so she only had one choice which was to run out of the room and find someone to help her.

She swung the door open and sprinted down the hallway past the other employee's rooms but no one was in site. Most of the employees were still working and those who weren't were typically found relaxing by the pool or at the karaoke bar. Neither of those locations was close by. She ran down the corridor toward the security center, those people should know about this and they could help her.

She burst through the glass doors that divided the accommodations from the offices and turned the corner to the main security check-in desk. As she raced around the corner she ran directly into an unwitting victim who had been heading in the opposite direction. Due to her speed, the impact of running headlong into the man's midriff sent her sprawling backward onto the floor. The startled man looked down at her writhing around, tears flowing down her face and covered from head to toe in blood. Clearly, she was in some kind of trouble.

"Are you OK? What happened? My name is Padraig," he said as he knelt down and offered a hand to help her get back to her feet. Suddenly aware of her state, Edith modestly pulled the robe tightly around herself as she got back on her feet without using the offer of his steadying hand. Danny who until now had escaped her notice stepped forward and repeated Padraig's initial stunned remarks.

"My shower," Edith said as she stoically checked her emotions "it is pouring nothing but blood out. No water. I didn't know what to do." As the last part of her explanation left her lips, her will weakened and the tears began to flow again. Padraig felt an instinctive need to embrace her but he couldn't overcome his stronger sense of reservedness. Danny had no such qualms. He gently reached his arm around Edith. She sunk her head into his shoulder and wept uncontrollably. Danny looked over her head to Padraig as if to say 'this is how you comfort someone you cold bastard.' Padraig put his hands in his back pockets awkwardly. He nodded repeatedly as he tried to convince himself that next time he ran into a hysterical person he would handle himself better.

"Well aren't you going to tell security ?" asked Danny.
Padraig hesitated for a second as it dawned on him that Danny had

risen from his usual role as sidekick and taken command of the situation. "Yes," he said, "I'll go now."

Dr. Barry Pargiter sat alone in the spacious water treatment laboratory. The room was equipped to accommodate 100 scientists each with their own workstation, computer, and a portable white plastic cabinet full of conical flasks, test tubes, and variously sized Bunsen burners. It was designed to be a dual purpose lab. It was supposed to host regular tests of water quality conducted by staff members, as well as seminars for visiting student groups the Entertainment Department of Aqua Monde believed the island would attract.

Today, Pargiter, a retirement-aged Oxford graduate from Southeastern England, was alone. His employees were waiting for engineers to finish repairs to the pumps that were essential to the desalination. The scientist was wearing his pristine white lab coat but work was the last thing on his mind. Technically, he had completed his days' work. A simple experiment to test the ice extracted from the aquifer. It's resistance to liquefaction had prompted some of his team to suggest the water contained impurities. Pargiter had tested the theory by simply warming the small chunk of ice in a conical flask. As he had anticipated, the ice melted into refreshing looking water.

He was sitting on his high stool enjoying an episode of 'Monty Python' on his IPad. The conical flask full of water was to his left. He found the show to be amusing. As he chuckled, wrinkles gave definition to every area of his thin and aged face. His hair was a mop of thick white curly hair which gave a hint as to his bohemian styled past.

Pargiter felt more at home in the lab than in the staff studio that he found to be stuffy. He also enjoyed the isolation that the science center provided. That silence was about to be disrupted by two unexpected visitors. The sound of the metal door at the back of the lab swinging open and hitting a wayward chair startled Pargiter. He stood up to see Cathy Furman and Kevin Newman marching towards him. Furman looked more steely-eyed than usual while Newman as ever looked in a daze.

"Can I help you?" asked Pargiter firmly as if addressing unwelcome intruders.
"Yes you can switch the water off and establish where the contamination occurred," said Furman in an equally cold tone of voice.
"Contamination?"
"Yes," said Newman, "Bloodied water is bellowing out of showers and wash basins all over the resort. While you were enjoying John Cleese on TV, someone crept in and contaminated the water supply."
"We need to find the source of the contamination right away," Furman demanded.

Pargiter reached down and reluctantly shut off his TV show as if to signal his realization that some work needed to be done. "That is quite out of the question," he said.
"What did you say?" asked Furman.
"I said it will be quite impossible to establish how the shower water was contaminated with blood."
"And why is that?" asked Newman.
"Because we're not in Liberia and if we were we could go and take a look at the water treatment plant there. Since we're not in Liberia I have no idea because the water you're talking about is the water we shipped in from that country and pumped directly into the water pipes here."
"The water has to go through a purification process," said Newman "or have you thrown the rule book out of the window Pargiter?"
"The drinking water has to go through that and incidentally the health and safety department only implemented that rule because they were assuming the drinking water would have been derived from ocean water. The water we're talking about isn't drinking water. It's water for bathing, and swimming," said Pargiter.
"Swimming ?" said Furman in horror.
"Yes swimming," replied Pargiter with a smile "but don't worry we don't change the pool water until tomorrow so it will keep its blue color for another day." He winked mockingly at her then turned and walked over to his desk where a laptop awaited him.

Pargiter started typing frantically while his visitors looked on. Furman looked at Newman with disgust "Do any of your employees have even the vaguest respect for you?" she asked. Newman didn't reply. "Have you fired that girl yet?" Furman asked.
"I was going to but then I got sidetracked with this."

"That should do it," said Pargiter as he stepped away from his desk.
"That should do what?" asked Furman.
"I have set lines up to draw back any remaining water from the supply pipes. It will take a few hours to drain it and then we'll have to run a cleaning agent through. We don't want any nasty little germs lingering in the system."
"How long will that take?" asked Newman.
"No more than 24 hours."
"24 hours isn't good enough," said Furman.
"Unless you want your guests bathing in a pinky foam possibly containing hepatitis, then it is something you'll have to put up with I am afraid."
"Boyle will have a conniption fit," blurted Newman.
"Well," said Pargiter "The recovery time for that is a lot quicker than for a fatal disease."
"There must be some other way to provide running water in the meantime," Furman proposed to Newman having decided that Pargiter was likely to remain less than helpful.
"We have bottles but if the pipes are out of action there isn't anything we can do," he said looking to Pargiter for affirmation "is there?"
"Well," said Pargiter as he switched the TV show on and sat on his stool "You might want to find yourself a few bottles of mineral water and a good sized bucket."

Newman and Furman left furiously without a word. Pargiter chuckled to himself. Feeling a little parched he reached out for the conical flask while he kept his eyes firmly fixed on his screen. He brought the flask to his lips and began to gulp as he anticipated a cool mouthful of water. But, no liquid was forthcoming. Puzzled he lowered the flask and glanced down at it. As he did so, he became aware of a chill in the palm of his hand. To his astonishment, the water in the flask had resolidified. The contents of the flask had spontaneously formed into solid ice.

"Jumping Jehoshaphat!" he exclaimed as the bitterly cold glass receptacle slipped from his grasp and smashed on the floor. Upon impact, the contents dissolved into a small puddle. "What have we here?" he asked himself in stunned amazement.

The "Mid Atlantic" canteen was largely empty aside from a few janitors mopping and waitresses waiting in vain for the chance to get tip money from guests who weren't likely to arrive. The news that the whole island would have to endure 24 hours without running water had caused a commotion. Long lines had formed at the cleaning supply store rooms as word had spread that free buckets were being distributed. The intent was for people to fill them with water from drinking fountains and then do their best to follow their usual cleaning rituals without the assistance of shower heads or faucets.

Edith Ndakolo had been provided with several liters of drinking water by the sympathetic staff in the security center. She was now feeling fresh and was ready to forget her unpleasant bathing experience. She sat in one of the small booths that formed a perimeter around the restaurant. She was talking about Namibia, her favorite topic, with her newly found friends Danny and Padraig. Danny sat opposite her and was clearly the target of most of her conversation as Padraig did his best to pay attention whilst being cognisant of the fact that she seemed less interested in speaking to him.

The trio were easy for Anne Hyeron to spot as she came in down the stairwell that linked the dining area to the upstairs bar. She had been scouring the resort for hours trying to find the English journalists. As she approached, she was surprised to see them in the company of the customer service representative that she had earlier fallen foul of. "What is she doing here ?" asked Anne. Edith rolled her eyes and looked down at the table. Danny, unaware of their earlier encounter, had a puzzled look on his face but it fell to Padraig to speak. "She had a bloody awful day," was his response.

He expected a chuckle from Danny and Edith but neither was amused. Glad of the opportunity to stop crowding their conversation, he rose from his chair and led Anne away from the table. "Do you know where that maintenance guy from the boat might be?" he

asked her. Anne had an entirely different topic on her mind "never mind about him" she said dismissively "I need you to write a story. We've found some ancient cave paintings and we need to get the story out before AM Corp demolishes the place."
"Cave paintings ?" Padraig was surprised at her suggestion "Erm I think you're mistaking me for the guy from The National Geographic. I am trying to work a story about someone contaminating water systems with someone or somethings' blood right now. The cave painting gig is going to have to wait."
"This isn't a joke," Anne said "This is evidence of a civilization that no one knew existed. There could be priceless artifacts and it's in the way of a chance for Wall Street to make some money. Isn't that a story?"

Padraig was impressed by her passion. Given the option between interrupting Danny and Edith's increasingly intimate chat and humoring the Floridian archaeologist, his decision was an easy one. "OK," he said, "I'll take a look and I'll put something together."
"We need to go there now," said Anne. Without giving him a chance to protest, she grabbed his hand and led him through the canteen towards the stairwell. As they started to climb the steps, loud footsteps coming from the opposite direction caught their attention. Up ahead was Beauchamp.

"Padraig," he yelled, "we've got him."
"Anne," Padraig said, "I will come with you to see your cave paintings."
Anne pushed him away. "You jerk."
"Anne," he pleaded "I will. I really will but I've got to go right now and speak to this guy about another story. Don't be mad."
"Just go," she said. Her face was full of fury but Padraig wanted to speak to Flomo before anyone realized he was no more than a journalist and not a secret service agent.
"I'll be back. I promise." Anne smirked as he patted her on the shoulder and scurried excitedly up the stairs.

Beauchamp led the way as they passed through the empty bar and into the main entrance hall of the resort. A huge fountain blasting showers of water 30 feet into the air was the centerpiece of the glass-domed structure. The walls were adorned with an array of seashells of every size and color. The handrails on the upper deck were designed to look like a line of flamingos with a beak to the back-of-the-head arrangement so the tops of the heads provided a banister of sorts. Beauchamp directed Padraig onto one of the two escalators that transported guests and workers between the floors. They rode to the ground floor then silently marched around the waterfall towards a neon pink door.

Beauchamp stared into the iris scanner. As was typical, it failed to respond. Perturbed, he held his ID card up to a magnetic stripe reader in the center of the door. It silently slid open. They walked through the doorway and Padraig realized that it was a back entrance into the security zone.

The cyborg Polar bear was guarding the entrance by himself. The security guard who normally manned the front desk was now standing next to a heavy-duty steel door across from the interview room. It looked like one of those giant valve doors you see on submarines in Steven Seagal movies, thought Padraig.
The guard was holding a handgun against his chest with his back firmly pressed against the door. Padraig walked towards the guard.
"I take it our terrorist is inside ?" the guard looked toward Beauchamp for permission to speak. Beauchamp nodded his head and in turn, the guard gave an affirmation nod to Padraig.

"Let's go in shall we?" said Beauchamp. As he reached for the door handle the guard stepped away and directed his pistol towards the room.
"Hold on," said Padraig, "I thought we agreed that I could interrogate him. Alone."
"Well," said Beauchamp "I agreed that we would use your methods but as Security Chief of this island I have a duty to be present when we are discussing matters that affect the safety of our guests."
"Look, Bob," Padraig put a firm hand on the Security Chiefs soldier "You know how people like me operate. We do what we have to but we get the job done. You are someone who needs to keep your hands clean. I don't want to implicate you in anything . . . unsavory that I may have to do in order to get this guy to talk. Do you get what I am

saying?" Beauchamp's lips twitched as he thought about what Padraig had just said. He rubbed his chin and exchanged looks with the security guard before finally standing tall and looking Padraig directly in the eye.
"I have your word that we can expect a full report on anything you learn from this suspect?"
"Of course," said Padraig "I will give you a full report."
"You won't go too overboard will you?" Beauchamp asked nervously.
"Overboard?"
"You won't" Beauchamp looked over his shoulder to make sure no one else was in the vicinity before whispering "you won't kill him." Padraig was stunned but maintained his composure and whispered back "I won't kill him . . . unless you need me to."
"I don't think that will be necessary . . . At this juncture you understand?"
"Good," replied Padraig with a smile "then without further ado I think I will get started. Gentlemen."

He pushed past the security duo and opened the door. Inside Flomo was sitting at a small rectangular table. He was still wearing his AM uniform and was hunched over the desk staring at the bare tabletop. He didn't look up until Padraig firmly slammed the door shut.
"You!" said Flomo. A grin spread across his face.
"You look happy to see me," said Padraig as he sat down on the molded plastic chair on the other side of the desk.
"No man I am not happy I just think it is funny," said Flomo.
"Funny?" Padraig was perplexed.
"I guess you are going to tell me that you are not an FBI agent," said Flomo.
"I am not an FBI agent," said Padraig.
Flomo roared with laughter. He slapped his hand on the desk three times as he burst into hysterics.
"I am glad that you are so amused by me," said Padraig.
Flomo regained his composure and sat up straight in his chair. He wiped the tears that had formed during his hysterics onto his sleeve.
"I am sorry man," Flomo said, "you are just the worst undercover agent ever."
"That's because I am not an undercover agent or a spy. I am a

journalist. I work for Knox Media."

Flomos smile disappeared and a look of rage spread across his face as he reached across the table and grabbed Padraig by his throat. "If you are a journalist then why the hell are these people telling me that you are going to come here and torture me huh ?" The grip on Padraig's throat was tightening. He tried to pull Flomo's hand away but his fingers were like a vice. Flomo slowly rose from his chair as he pressed his finger deep into the journalist's skin. "Who are you?" asked Flomo menacingly before pushing Padraig flat on his back onto the cold stone floor. Padraig cracked his skull against the ground.

Flomo turned his back and began to pace the room as the journalist slowly crawled to his feet. With Flomo's back turned, Padraig felt a strong urge to grab the small table and hurl it at him. But as he rubbed his throat, his journalistic longing to uncover the truth overtook his desire for retaliation.

"Look," said Padraig "Honest to God. I am a bloody journalist. These idiots think I am a spy because you got me and Danny wondering about things and we started snooping around when we got here."
Flomo turned to look at Padraig. The site of the Englishman wincing at the pain caused by his bumped head convinced him that Padraig was telling the truth.
"You are right," said Flomo "you are too weak to be in the FBI." Flomo sat down at the table and gestured for Padraig to do the same.
"If it is all the same to you," said Padraig "I would prefer to stand." He glanced down at his chair which was still laying on the floor.
"Your choice," said Flomo.

"So tell me," said Padraig "what is with the blood? I saw something similar in Monrovia. Is it some kind of black magic sacrifice or something?"
"What the hell?" said Flomo indignantly, "No Dr. Livingstone, you do not have to come here and civilize those of us on the dark continent. It is not witchcraft you prat."
"Prat?" said Padraig "I haven't had anyone call me that in years."

"Really?" said Flomo "That's surprising."
"So what is with the blood then?"
"If I tell you," said Flomo "they will kill you if they know that you know."
"Who will kill me?"
"The government in Liberia, the people who built this place, take your pick."
"Why will they kill me?" asked Padraig. He felt he was finally starting to make progress. He bent down and put his chair upright. He sat down and shuffled his way to the edge of the table. "Why will they kill me Flomo?"
"The same reason they will kill me. Because money is involved. Big money," replied the Liberian.
"How much money?"
"How long is a piece of string," snapped Flomo. "This island cost billions to build but they were allowed to do it because it will make trillions and it will bring fresh water to West Africa. But imagine if it was all a lie."
"A lie?"
"A lie. Made up. Fake."
"I don't get you," said Padraig "we're here! How can it be fake?"
"They desalinate water here and ship it to Africa right?" said Flomo.
"Right," replied Padraig.
"You tell me you saw a water plant in Monrovia with water contaminated by blood. Today a ship arrives from Liberia to this island and now the water here is contaminated by blood. Who is giving water to who Mr. Coyle?"
Padraig slumped back on his chair looking puzzled. "You mean that they are stealing water from Africa to bring to this resort? But they have been showing ships coming from here pumping fresh water into the Monrovia reservoirs. How do you explain that?"
"You have never heard of thieves who steal things and return to town the next day as merchants selling the same items back to the victims?"
"Surely people would notice?"
"Of course they notice but who would believe a guy on the street?"

"So you killed a bunch of animals and dumped their bodies in the city water system to try and draw attention to this ?" asked Padraig.

"I didn't kill any animals," said Flomo quietly "the animals North of the city are dying because the rivers are being sucked dry to bring water to this place. The rice fields are dry. The farmers are starving. The rich come here and bathe in hot tubs with the water that a year ago was used to irrigate the fields of my country."

"This is hard to believe," said Padraig "can you provide me with any evidence?"

Flomo threw his hands into the air in exasperation "You were on the ship. The tanks were full after LEAVING Africa. You saw the blood at the water plant. You saw the same water here after it came on our ship! You are the journalist! You fill in the blanks."

A loud rap of knuckles on the door caught both men's attention.

"Come in," shouted Padraig.

The door opened and Beauchamp poked his head in. "How are things going?" he asked.

Padraig stood up and pushed his chair under the table. "He is a tough one to crack. Had to rough him up a bit but he'll talk," said Padraig. He had his back to Beauchamp and unseen by the security officer he winked at the prisoner. Flomo nodded in acknowledgment.

Padraig turned and briskly marched to the door "give him some food then leave him alone to stew on things until I return."

"What should I tell my boss?" asked Beauchamp.

"If you want my help you are going to have to play along with me," said Padraig "make something up." He patted Beauchamp on the back as he exited the room.

The Security Chief stared at Flomo. The Liberian tried to avoid his gaze but as he looked towards the ceiling he could sense that Beauchamp was transfixed upon him. After a few more seconds of uncomfortable silence, he stared back at him and exclaimed "What?" Beauchamp caught off guard sheepishly replied, "I hope he wasn't too rough with you." He turned without waiting for a reaction and slammed the door behind him. Flomo looked at his watch. It was mid-afternoon. He hoped Padraig would get the story into the media in time for the grand opening when the whole world would be watching.

BETRAYAL

Henrik forcefully marched through the aquarium tunnel towards the communications center. It was a 10-foot cylindrical, glass pipe that passed through the center of the marine life sanctuary. A menacing lemon shark seemed to grin at him as he scurried by. Aqua Monde had two separate telecommunication centers; one for guests to use and the other was reserved for staff. Guest telephone booths charged $10 per minute, staff telephone booths were free. The Norwegian was nothing if not frugal. Henrik used the iris scan to access the staff telecommunication center. The room was located midway between the 'Mid Atlantic' restaurant and the staff accommodations.

He was alone. There were 10 glass desks along three of the walls, with a computer and telephone sitting on top of each one. Frosted glass barriers reaching from the floor to the ceiling offered a degree of privacy for people using the booths. The walls and floor were decorated with alternating sky blue, and white plastic tiles. The ceiling consisted of frosted glass tiles that accentuated the bright sunlight illuminating the room from above.

Henrik grabbed the nearest phone. He began dialing the international code for Switzerland before realizing the phone line was dead. He held the phone tightly to his right ear while repeatedly pressing the receiver with his left hand. After persevering for a minute, he hung on the telephone and moved on to the next terminal. He put the phone to his ear but there was no dial tone. Henrik frantically raced around the room picking up random telephones desperately trying to find one that worked. None of the phones were working. "Dammit." Henrik knew he didn't have enough money on his debit card to pay for a call on one of the guest telephones. He clenched his teeth together in frustration realizing how important it was for him to contact UNESCO.

"Is everything okay?" Henrik looked up, Kevin Newman was standing in the doorway. He was the last person Henrik wanted to see. Henrik, like the rest of his team, felt Kevin was the cause of all their problems.
"I'm fine, I was just trying to make a phone call. It wasn't anything

important," said Henrik despondently. Kevin raised an eyebrow. He could see from Henrik's demeanor that the young Swedish scientist was upset. He suspected it had something to do with the excavation site. Despite his unpopularity with the scientists, Kevin felt that Henrik would have given him an answer if he had been upset about something other than the dig.

"Look," said Kevin quietly "I can see you're upset. I know you guys are upset with me but I haven't changed and you can still trust me. Is there a problem at the dig? It's okay we can talk freely, no one else is around. Henrik, trust me."
Henrik looked directly at Kevin. He didn't look like a liar. He sounded sincere and despite Henrik's general loathing of him, he felt he had no choice but to trust him.
"Yes," said Henrik "we found something, something important."
Kevin nervously looked over his shoulder to make sure they were alone. Satisfied that no one else was around, Kevin made his way into the room and stopped within whispering distance of Henrik.
"What is it,?" asked Kevin excitedly "what did you find?"
"Anne will kill me if I tell you," said Henrik dejectedly.
"For goodness sake, what do you think I am? I am a scientist. I was working on archaeological digs before you were born. I recruited Anne, I recruited all of them. Do you really think I would do anything to jeopardize the dig?"

Henrik stared deeply into Kevin's eyes. The older man stared back at him. He didn't blink, he didn't frown, he seemed confident, he seemed honest. Henrik took a deep breath and began to speak. "We found some cave paintings."
Kevin stepped back, he was stunned. "Cave paintings?" He said.
"Yes," said Henrik "something very ancient. They look like Egyptian hieroglyphs except they have images rather than characters. They seem to tell a story, but I don't know what! We think it's about some kind of water or ice based deity"
"So if you just made this amazing discovery, what are you doing here?" Said Kevin.
"Anne thinks the company will try to close down the dig because it will cost them too much money to allow us to complete a full archaeological survey. She told me to call UNESCO and get the

word out so that the company would have no choice but to let us finish the dig."
"Well," said Kevin "you won't be able to call anyone right now because they lost power at the transmission tower. It had something to do with an electrical storm a few hours ago. The thing is supposed to be storm proof but like everything here it isn't all that it's cracked up to be." Henrik sighed deeply and raised his hands to his face.
"When will it be working again?" He asked.
"Could be hours," said Kevin flippantly "but don't worry I can take care of this."

Kevin unclipped his walkie-talkie from his belt. He held it to his mouth, pressed the transmission button and began to speak.
"This is Kevin Newman," he said, "I'm at the staff telecommunication bureau and I need a security officer down here right now."
"What are we going to do?" Asked Henrik.
"Don't worry I have a plan," said Kevin as a broad smile spread across his face. The sound of footsteps echoed down the corridor and within seconds a security officer holding an automatic weapon marched into the room. Kevin stepped away from Henrik. Turning to the security guard he pointed at Henrik. "Arrest this man," commanded Kevin "take him to a detention cell, don't let him speak to anyone. He is a security threat."

Henrik backed away. His jaw dropped as his heart sank. He should have stuck with his instincts and not trusted Kevin. He had jeopardized the whole project. "You lied to me. You told me you have been doing this for years. Why?"
Kevin smiled. "I wasted the best years of my life chasing dusty relics and rotting corpses. I never got married, never had a family and never had a penny to my name. What kind of life is that?" asked Kevin. "You will thank me one-day Henrik, I'm saving you from the life that I have had." Henrik smirked. He gave Kevin one last soul-searching glare before compliantly marching down the hallway with a gun at his back.

"Here they come," said Edith as she wearily resigned herself to an afternoon with the unhappy guests. Danny stood silently beside her as the group of Aqua Monde's first visitors trudged their way across the restaurant towards their unenthusiastic African guide. Billy Bradshaw was at the front of the group and in his own mind was the unofficial spokesman. Mike Patel followed close behind, curious to see the latest episode in the Billy Bradshaw saga. He did not have to wait long to see Billy vocalize his latest complaint.

"Oi," yelled Billy "this ain't what we bleeding signed on for. We have been drinking bottled water and I can't even flush the bog when I take a dump." Mike Patel stopped in his tracks to allow a respectable distance between him and Bradshaw who had embarrassed himself once again. Danny chuckled only to earn a disapproving glance from Edith, who as ever attempted to keep her composure.
"Well Mr. Bradshaw," she said, "I have some wonderful news. Our talented water maintenance crew have fixed the problem and the water will be up and running in just a few minutes." She smiled as the majority of the guests gave her a polite round of applause.

Billy had not expected the problem to be solved so quickly and stood silently as his main conversation piece had just been made redundant. Danny, feeling out of place, took ahold of the camera hanging around his neck and started taking snapshots of the guests. He silently slid away from the group as he attempted to capture the scene.

Hugh Pompidou, who was lingering at the back of the group, gave Danny a disapproving glare. He hadn't washed or changed his clothes since arriving. He did not want to be photographed looking anything less than his best. Pompidou had not been overseas for 20 years. His last trip had been a rather more luxurious affair. In his younger days, Pompidou took many cruises in the Mediterranean with his longtime companion Tim Richardson. He hadn't been abroad since Richardson died during a trip to Dubrovnik in 1991. He felt self-conscious traveling alone. It had taken his neighbor, Mike Patel several months to convince him to come on this trip. Based on the events of the first few days, Pompidou was starting to regret that decision. "Madam," he said. No one heard him so he jostled his way

through the group until he found himself between his neighbor and Bradshaw at the head of the party. "Excuse me," he mumbled. Edith stepped closer to him so she could hear him clearly over the excited conversation of the rest of his party. Edith took hold of his arm as she lent towards him.
"Yes Mr. Pompidou," she said, "can I help you with something?"
"Well I don't want to be a nuisance," said the aging Texan "I do feel a little faint. Perhaps it's all this excitement, I am not sure. I would like to sit down for a minute or two."
"Of course," said Edith " we are going to take a nice little break now in the restaurant area. Let's take a seat over here." Pompidou nodded his consent as Edith slowly led him towards the nearest booth.

Mike gestured to his wife Gita to follow the old man. He wasn't eager to speak to him as much as he was keen to sit down with him before anyone less desirable burdened him with inane conversation. Edith helped Pompidou onto the bench seat on one side of the booth. Gita and Mike Patel hurriedly scrambled onto the bench on the other side of the table.

Edith smiled "Oh, I see you have some friends. Can I get you all a drink?"
"My wife and I would both like a nice cup of tea, with some lemon, a small bit of sugar but no milk." He raised his finger in the air as he emphasized the last part of his order.
"And how about you Mr. Pompidou," asked Edith "what would you like to drink?"
"Well it is a bit dull but I would rather like a glass of water."
"That is not dull at all," replied Edith with false sincerity "would you also like a lemon with that?"
"No, not really. I am not a big fan of citrus fruits to be perfectly honest. Oh and also I do not want any ice," said Pompidou "cold drinks make me rather quick." Edith smiled before turning and walking towards the bar area at the far side of the room.

The other guests had shuffled into the 1950s Americana style booths that lined the perimeter of the restaurant. Danny, who had been quietly taking pictures for the past few minutes, stood quietly by the stairwell that led to the main entrance hall. He had enjoyed his

afternoon with Edith but his new-found friend was otherwise engaged. The sound of rapid footsteps caught his attention. He spun around and saw Padraig scurrying down the stairs towards him. Danny was ready to tell Padraig all about his romantic afternoon in the restaurant. Before a word left his mouth Padraig was barking commands.
"I spoke to that bloke from the ship," whispered Padraig as he reached the ground level "there is something big going on here. We were right. The boat we came in on was bringing water and apparently, these people have been sucking Liberia dry for months."

Danny quickly realized that Padraig would have no interest in talking about his prospects for forming a romantic attachment with Edith. He didn't mind though. Padraig was always fun to hang around with when he was on a mission.
"So what is the plan?" Asked Danny.
"The plan is that we find our pissy little archaeologist friend and have her get us into that water processing plant so we can get enough evidence to write a story in Sunday's paper." Padraig patted Danny on the shoulder before turning and running back up the stairs. He was halfway to the top when he realized Danny had not followed him. "Well, come on what are you waiting for?" Danny looked across the restaurant towards Edith hoping for a chance to wave goodbye. She was tied up in conversation with Mike Patel. Disappointedly Danny turned and followed Padraig up the stairwell.

The journalists quickly reached the main entrance hall. It was eerily silent. No one was about and even the elevator was stationary. The flamingos serving as handrails seemed to be silently watching her. The fastest way to the dig site was to pass through the security center. Padraig tried to use his magnetic room key to open the neon pink door that led to the security center. The door was unresponsive. From the glass doorway beneath the escalator, Anne suddenly appeared and came running towards them. She was sweating and struggling to catch her breath. "Oh my God," she mumbled before slouching over and taking several deep breaths. Padraig and Danny bewilderedly exchanged glances. Anne stood up straight, placed her hands on her hips and started walking in circles with their head tilted back as she attempted to regulate her breathing.

"You know you should probably work out a bit more," said Padraig," as Anne finally regained her composure. She responded with a sarcastic grin and then took one last deep breath before raising her arms as if to form a huddle. Danny and Padraig again exchanged confused looks before reciprocating. The three of them closed in shoulder to shoulder as if they were having a team talk.

"Okay," whispered Anne "here is the deal. We need you guys to call your boss and get the story out about these ancient cave paintings that we have found. I sent Henrik to try and call UNESCO but he never came back. I just overheard a security officer saying that they have him locked up." Padraig didn't believe her. He suspected she was creating a fantastic tale to get their help. "They arrested him?" Said Padraig suspiciously, "why would they arrest him for telling UNESCO that you found a bunch of caveman paintings?"

Anne was irritated, she stamped on Padraig's foot. Stunned, Padraig broke away from the huddle and bent down to touch his throbbing big toe. " Seriously are you some kind of psycho?" he said angrily. Anne stepped towards him and slammed the palm of her right hand into his chest. "No I am not a psycho but I will become a psycho if you don't stop pissing me off. They have Henrik locked up, I don't know why but I think it must have something to do with the cave paintings." Padraig could tell that she was telling the truth or at least that she believed she was telling the truth.

"Fine," he said "let's say you're right and you heard the guard say this, maybe he was pulling your leg. You are pretty easily wound up you know." A second and more forceful palm to the chest let him know that she disagreed. Danny could see that this conversation was going nowhere. He grabbed Anne by the shoulder and pulled her back from Padraig. Anne was about to hit Danny but changed her mind as he began to speak. "Padraig," said Danny, "you are the one telling me that these people are siphoning water from Africa and marketing this place as a miracle cure for Africa's water shortages. Isn't it possible that they have some other stuff going on too?" Anne thought about smiling at Danny but instead chose to fix a dastardly glare on Padraig.

Danny, irritated with his friend for his insensitivity towards Edith earlier in the day also looked menacingly at his colleague. Padraig desperately wanted to make some kind of wisecrack to break the tension but he didn't think either of them were in the mood for further delays.

"Okay," said Padraig "here is what we can do. Anne, get us into the water treatment facility so we can get some hard evidence. Like it or not, our boss is going to be much more likely to print a story about corrupt corporations causing droughts in Africa than she is to publish a story about archaeology. However, if you help us we will help you. Danny has his camera and technically he is a freelance. We could have those pictures in the English tabloids tomorrow. How does that sound?"

"That sounds like the first sensible thing you have said all day," said Anne.

Flomo was sitting in his cell patiently waiting for Padraig to expose his corporate nemesis. He sat at the table just as Padraig had left him. He intended to sit at that spot until someone put an end to Aqua Monde Corporation. With a noisy clank, the cell door opened. In walked a security guard holding a tray of food and drink. The plate of mashed potato and meatloaf looked less than appetizing. Flomo was pleased to have an opportunity to show his defiance to one of the guards. The guard placed the tray on the table. As he turned and headed back to the door, Flomo firmly grabbed the tray with both hands and flung it against the nearest cell wall. Chunks of watery mashed potato slid slowly down to the floor. The guard turned and looked contemptuously at Flomo. "Nick," said the guard "come in here."

A second guard holding an automatic rifle marched into the room. He saw smashed glass, a pool of water, a broken plate and a heap of mashed potato on the ground. Having contemplated the spectacle he briskly marched towards the desk where Flomo sat. As the Liberian looked up at him, he thrust the butt of his rifle into the prisoner's face. As the guards turned to leave, Flomo tasted blood seeping from his nose into the back of his mouth. He put his hands to his face. His nose had immediately become swollen. Judging from the pain, his nose was broken.

With a loud clank the cell door closed and Flomo was alone again. In the hallway outside, the guard who had struck Flomo put his gun down on the food cart and picked up the remaining tray. His colleague opened the cell door opposite Flomo's. As it swung open he saw Henrik sitting at a table identical to the one Flomo had in his cell. Unlike the Liberian, Henrik excitedly sat up when he saw the plate of food headed in his direction.

"Wow, thanks guys," he said with genuine enthusiasm "I was starting to get really hungry in here." The guard placed the tray on his table without a word. He had been hoping for an excuse to rough up the Swedish prisoner but he left the cell silently. As the door closed, Henrik picked up his fork and started to devour his meal. He took a few bites of the meatloaf. Despite its rough texture he happily gobbled it down. He could feel the food lodging in his parched throat so he picked up a glass of water from his tray and took a long swig. The water had an unusual aftertaste. It was pleasant enough but slightly odd tasting.

On the tray next to the plate was a bottle from which the water had come. He picked up the bottle to read the label. It said "Aqua Monde natural volcanic spring water." Henrik was impressed. He had heard a lot about the restorative qualities of the volcanic mineral water his employers had found close to the archaeological dig site. This was the first time he had tried it. He looked down at his plate of food. As the first few mouthfuls slowly made their way towards his stomach the remaining food suddenly looked less appetizing. He finished his drink and gave the rest of the meal a pass. He savored the peculiar water's taste for a second before an odd sensation unsettled him.

As the last gulp of water passed through his throat it felt incredibly cool, ice cold, colder than anything he had ever consumed before. The chilling sensation did not pass and grew stronger and more widespread. He could feel a frigid surge spreading through his thorax and down into his chest. As the cold feeling moved through his body, his lungs seemed to lose their capacity to fill with air. Henrik stood up from the table and put his hands to his chest. He could feel something passing through his veins into his arms and legs. It was uncomfortable but it was becoming painful. All the while his breathing became more rapid and his breaths shallower. He knew the guards were just outside. He could hear their mumbles. He tried to call for help but he didn't find the strength to vocalize his thoughts.

He stumbled towards the door, his body gripped by unexplained pain. As he reached the metal door he fell to his knees. His mouth was open but something was preventing him from inhaling air. He put his hands to his throat and tried to squeeze the unseen obstacle from his neck. It was to no avail. He stretched a hand towards the door.
But before his hand touched the metal his whole arm went numb. He could faintly feel some kind of sensation, a throbbing deep inside his flesh but he could not move his limb. The numb sensation shot up

through his upper arm across his shoulders and down into his other arm. He felt something deep inside him race from the top of his head to the tips of his toes. He was helpless. He could not breathe, he could not move, all he could do was listen to the faint vibrations of his heartbeat. He knew that he was about to die. He could do nothing to prevent it. The people who might have helped were on the other side of a five-inch thick steel door. For one split second, Henrik realized he could no longer hear his own heartbeat, but that thought was his last. Henrik was dead.

Anne, Danny, and Padraig stood at the back entrance door to the desalination plant. Anne retrieved her staff ID card from her jeans back pocket and placed it over the magnetic card reader located to the left of the metallic white door. The entrance was unmarked. Padraig silently wondered how Anne and the other stuff found their way around the complex since practically everything was whitewashed and featureless.

"Here we go!" said Anne. She was nervous that security may have blocked her card access when they decided to imprison Henrik. After a split second delay, that felt like an eternity, the metallic door slid upwards to reveal a seemingly deserted hallway. At the far end of the corridor was a glass door beyond which appeared to be a laboratory. It was the only doorway in the hallway, so to get anywhere else the trio would have to pass through the lab.

"What do we do if someone is in?" asked Danny. Anne didn't feel the need to ask the same question but like Danny, she looked up at Padraig for an answer. Padraig pursed his lips and stared towards the ceiling as if in deep thought while his cohorts patiently waited for a response.
"Danny," said Padraig finally "you stay here so if anyone comes this way looking for us you can try to delay them and give us a heads' up."
Danny did not mind taking orders but didn't like imprecise instructions "what do you mean delay them and give you a heads up?" He asked indignantly. Padraig suspected that they would have very little time to look for evidence to back up Flomo's allegations and he didn't want to waste a lot of time helping Danny formulate an action plan.
"You are a big boy, you figure it out. Anne, you come with me because we may need your card once we get past that door."

Danny attempted to protest but Padraig and Anne were already running down the hallway towards the glass door. He resigned himself to being a watchdog, leant his back against the wall, then his legs, and slowly slid down until he was sitting on the floor. He had been on his feet all day. He decided that anyone finding him there would query his presence anyway so he may as well take the weight off his feet.

Meanwhile, Padraig and Anne peered through the glass door. They were looking into the main science laboratory. Despite the dozens of flickering PC screens, the room appeared to be empty. Unlike most of the other rooms in the complex, there was no magnetic card reader. As Padraig gently pressed his hand to the door he discovered that it was unlocked. He looked to Anne for reassurance but she responded with an uneasy shrug of the shoulders. Padraig knew that they had to search the lab but the silence made him uneasy. He took a deep breath and flung the door open. It was a swing door and as it swung back towards him he stretched his arm out to stop it from hitting him. Anne ducked under his arm and stepped into the room.

"Can I help you?" Sitting on a stall with his back to the wall to the left side of the doorway was Dr. Barry Pargiter. Anne felt sure he must have heard them talking in the hallway given his proximity to the door. She felt defeated. She put her hands on her hips, dramatically rolled her eyes, and gave Padraig a look that let him know that he was to blame. Padraig ignored Anne entirely and decided his best course of action was to hope Pargiter had heard nothing.

"Yes I am here from security and I need to conduct an inspection of your laboratory." Pargiter laughed mockingly. He rubbed his chin as he rose from his stall "I have to say I am a little disappointed. I thought I might run into you but I hoped you might be a little bit more creative than that." Padraig frowned. He was confused. He had no idea who Pargiter was so he wondered how the scientist knew him. "Excuse me," said Padraig who was intending to try and keep the pretense going "my name is Bobby Sandison and I am with corporate security. Now, are you going to cooperate? Or will I have to report you for insubordination?"

Pargiter shook his head and began to tut repeatedly. "You really are not very good at this, are you? I know exactly who you are, we all got an email when you and your friend started nosing around the complex." Pargiter picked up a sheet of paper from his desk. He handed it Padraig to prove his point. Padraig looked down at the paper and saw thumbnail-sized images of him and Danny in the center on what appeared to be an email from Beauchamp. Padraig knew the game was up. "Well as you can see it's not a particularly good likeness, they didn't get my best side," said Padraig hoping for a laugh from Anne. She wasn't impressed and another eye roll let him know it.

"Well," said Pargiter excitedly "I don't get a lot of visitors so now that you are here what was it that you were hoping to find out?"
"Well," said Padraig "to be perfectly honest I have reason to believe that this whole place, this whole setup is a fraud."
"Go on," said Pargiter expectantly.
"This operation, this plan to bring water to Africa is actually a scam and you people are stealing water from Liberia and bringing it here to fill up swimming pools for the rich and famous." Padraig had delivered his allegation under the assumption that Pargiter was implicit in the creation of the entire plan. He folded his arms waiting for the scientist to try and deny the charge.
"You are absolutely correct," said Pargiter "was there anything else?"
"Are you for real? Asked Anne angrily.
"Young lady," said Pargiter calmy "I am one of the few people in this entire place who is real."

Padraig realized that Pargiter was an intellectual type who liked to make his conversational counterparts work to elicit information from him. "Calm down Anne," said Padraig "why don't you tell me exactly what is going on here, and what your role is in all of this."

Pargiter had no love for Aqua Monde. He had been hired by the corporation at the behest of the UN for whom he had spent years developing new methods for desalination. He hoped to alleviate water shortages in the developing world. AM had spent billions on the island, but relatively little on the research lab that was essential to its creation. Pargiter had spent months working alone as AM claimed that they could not find sufficiently qualified candidates to assist him. Most of Pargiter's crew were junior scientists with little experience beyond undergraduate classrooms.

When he first began work for the corporation, he genuinely believed their explanations for the delays and technical problems that beset him. More recently, he had come to realize that AM lacked the means or the will to invest in science. Instead, they planned to pay for the research only after making billions through the resort. As far as the rest of the world knew, the finances were supposed to work the other way around. Thus far, the only progress that had been made in terms of drinking water production had been the discovery of the volcanic spring waters deep underground.

AM had been quick to recognize the marketing potential of spring water rich in nutrients harvested from ancient sources in the middle of the Atlantic Ocean. The AM advertising team had even branded the spring water as the water that the people of Atlantis once drank. In the US, the corporation was already running TV ads showing images of the mythic city being destroyed in a volcanic eruption. Actors portraying Atlanteans lamented the fact they would no longer be able to drink the purest drinking water in the world. Millions of bottles had been prepared for shipment but sales were not to commence until after the grand opening of the Aqua Monde resort.

Eventually, revenue from spring water and tourism would give Pargiter and his colleagues sufficient funding to establish a viable desalination plant that could serve Northwest Africa. Pargiter explained everything to Padraig, he had resigned himself to spending the rest of his career in his large but lonely lab. Padraig was amazed that Pargiter was so forthcoming.
"Well that was a lot easier than I expected," said Padraig.
"You should have a good story in your hands, young man," said Pargiter "which is important. I hear that a lot of seasoned journalists have been losing their jobs of late."
"Tell me about it," said Padraig wearily "half of my friends are having to make ends meet writing crap for clickbait websites. I don't want to end up writing articles about how to wipe your ass for the rest of my life. This story should keep me in the job for a couple of weeks at very least." Pargiter laughed.

"If you really want a scoop though" Pargiter continued "you should hang around for a bit. I am doing some electrolysis experiments on the water from the underground aquifers. It has curious properties the likes of which neither I nor anyone else has ever seen."
Padraig was too concerned with his corporate expose to get sidetracked with a science experiment. "I'll get back to you on that one," he said dismissively.

"Now young lady, may I ask how you wound up with this troublemaker," said Pargiter jokingly. "Don't you have enough things going on to keep you occupied at your archaeological dig site?"
"How did you know that I work at the archaeological site?" Anne was unnerved by the fact that this stranger seemed to know who she was.
"Oh come now young lady, we came in on the same ship together six months ago. You, me, and a number of stuffed suits. You stood out like a sore thumb" said Pargiter with a smile.

Anne was not as taken with the scientist as Padraig seemed to be.
"Well I have a question for you as it happens," said Anne.
"I am all ears," replied Pargiter.
"I was under the impression that desalination created a lot of waste products that could be harmful if dumped back into the ocean. I assume your plan is to dump the waste chemicals into the ocean once you have made your drinking water? So how does that tie-in with your Mr conscientious routine?" Anne pointed an accusatory finger at Pargiter as the second of her rhetorical questions left her mouth.

"Well, there is a benefit to having this place in the middle of the ocean far away from coastal fishing waters. It is because everyone wanted the water but nobody wanted the plant in their backyard." Pargiter delivered his response in an unapologetic, matter-of-fact tone. He sat back down on his stall and folded his arms defensively in anticipation of an angry response from the young archaeologist. Padraig beat her to the punch "Well hold on a minute," said the journalist "so I suppose you must have dumped all that blood and crap into the ocean that you drained from the water supply?" Anne winced at the thought of gallons of stagnant cow's blood billowing into the beautiful deep blue seas that surrounded their man-made island.

"Well," said Pargiter, directing his response to Anne "the powers-that-be obviously share your sentiments because they redirected all that nasty stuff elsewhere. They didn't think it would create a good impression for a big shareholder to arrive and find cows' eyeballs bouncing around in the surf." Anne liked the visual image of that even less than the previous one.

"So what did you do with it?" Asked Padraig.
"Our head of scientific research setup a drainage line to siphon it off to some kind of underground cavern close to the archaeological dig site." A cold shudder passed down Anne's spine as she processed the scientist's last statement. Kevin Newman, her despised former boss, was the head of science. Could he have found out about the cave from Henrik? Was that why Henrik was being detained in the security detention area? Was Newman going to sabotage her site and destroy a unique archaeological find?

"Where exactly did he say that this cavern was?" Asked Anne nervously. Padraig suddenly realized what Anne was thinking. "Surely they wouldn't do that?" he said.
"I wouldn't put anything past Newman," said Anne "he wouldn't want anyone else to steal his limelight." Pargiter had no idea what they were talking about but as someone who had had unpleasant dealings with Newman himself, he was keen to do what he could to help. "They didn't tell me the exact location," he said "they just told me they found some kind of old cave on the edge of the archaeological dig site that was a safety hazard. They are going to dump my byproducts in there and fill it in with concrete." Anne did not hang around to explain to Pargiter what was happening. The words had barely left his mouth and she was halfway down the hallway towards the door where they had left Danny waiting.

Padraig, feeling slightly embarrassed at her hasty departure but keen to follow, started to mumble some kind of explanation to Pargiter but the scientist waved him away. "I think you had better get after her," said Pargiter "she looks pretty upset and things might get a bit ugly." Padraig, like Anne before him, abruptly left without another word. He suddenly realized that Anne was probably right about Henrik being arrested. Padraig was in a precarious position. If Anne caused a scene and got herself arrested, it would leave him in a position where the two primary sources of his exposé were behind bars. He raced down the hallway. As the metallic door at the end of it slid upwards, he saw a bewildered looking Danny. He didn't have time for explanations, he just grabbed Danny by the arm and said: "come on."

DESTRUCTION

The restaurant area had become a hive of activity, Aqua Monde staff members were erecting eight feet high hoardings made of corrugated plastic featuring pictures of the resort. All of the advertising material featured the slogan 'Who said they weren't making land anymore?' Maintenance men were hanging studio lighting from the restaurant ceiling. Entertainment manager Cathy Furman was supervising the whole affair. She started barking orders, clipboard in hand, to anyone who was within five feet of her.

Edith wasn't sure what to do with her tour group. They would have been at the water park had the water supply not been disrupted most of the past 24 hours. In all of the commotion, she had been forgotten about and nobody seemed to realize that the first group of visitors were forming a rather negative impression of the resort. Edith had been trying to keep people entertained with light conversation about the weather and discussions of which celebrity visitors were likely to visit the island.

She had no inside knowledge about the VIP guests, but Mike Patel seemed fairly convinced that famous English soccer player Gary Davies would be in attendance. "I read it in the Bombay Gazette," he had said "I read it on the Internet every morning. It's a very good journal." Edith had Patel's words stuck in her head due to the fact he had felt the need to repeat himself several times to ensure that everyone would give him credit for his prediction if indeed the soccer star did show up. Edith started pacing around nervously. She feared Cathy Furman would give her a dressing down for allowing the bored guests to hang around in an area that currently more resembled a building site than a restaurant lounge. Conversely, she also feared how Furman would react if she attempted to take the group on a tour of the resort. She had received very little information from anyone since the water came back on. She had no idea what state of functionality the rest of the resort was in.

All of a sudden, Cathy Furman happened to notice Edith standing just a few feet away from her. "Shouldn't you be showing your tour group around the resort?"
"Well," said Edith nervously "I wanted to ask you about that because

I wasn't sure if everything was back up and running after the water problems."

Cathy's jaw dropped. She didn't immediately respond but tilted her head as her bulging eyes seemed to pop out of her skull. Edith was not sure if Cathy was expecting a response. She stared back blankly. Finally, Furman broke the stand-off "What have you been doing with these people all day?" She demanded to know.
"Well," said Edith "for most of the day we have been hanging out in here." As soon as the words left her mouth she knew that was the wrong thing to say. She also knew that whatever she said, Furman would have reacted as if it was the 'wrong thing to say.'

Furman broke out of her gaping mouth and tilted head position, and stood up straight to give Edith a lecture. "So you don't have a problem coming to me complaining when someone hurts your feelings or when your shower isn't functioning properly. But when it's time to do your actual job you are reduced to a quivering wreck incapable of speaking up for yourself." Furman seemed even angrier than Edith had expected her to be but she wasn't finished yet. "Do you know how many young girls we interviewed for these positions? How many people would love to have this opportunity and you stand around here, in a daydream letting our VIP guests fend for themselves in a restaurant that currently resembles a junkyard!" Furman finished her rebuke of Edith by placing her hands on her hips, tilting her head to one side and letting her jaw drop as if she were a frog waiting to catch a passing fly.

In reality, Furman had forgotten all about the tour group. She realized there was very little Edith could have been expected to do with the guests given the circumstances. But she also felt she could not allow an employee to think there were occasions when customer service levels should slip. Despite the fact that she was thousands of miles from home and lacked the means to leave the island, Edith contemplated telling Furman to 'stick' her job. Before she could make a decision one way or the other Furman began talking again.
"I suggest you take our weary travelers outside and ask them if they would like to have a swim in the outdoor pool."
"Yes miss, I mean ma'am, I mean ma'am," said Edith who had

decided to drop any ideas of a revolt and get on with her job as best she could.

Furman marched off to berate another worker while Edith sauntered over to her tour group who were still nestled in the restaurant booths. As she approached, Mike Patel stood and raised his right forefinger to his lips. The noisy group compliantly descended into silence. Satisfied with his work Patel sat down again. Edith smiled at him but as she did, she noticed that Hugh Pompidou was no longer sitting at Patel's table. "Thank you, Mr. Patel," said Edith "I see that Mr. Pompidou has gone, is everything okay?"
"Yes," said Patel "he went for a stroll he said he had a bit of rheumatism or something … it happens with old people." Edith smiled.

"Well, ladies and gentlemen if you would like to return to your rooms and fetch your bathing suits we can reconvene here in about 20 minutes and take a swim in our main pool."
For the first time since they arrived the tour group seemed genuinely excited. Edith was pleased to be the bearer of good news for a change. She stood proudly as the guests gathered their belongings and made their way towards the stairwell that led to the accommodations.

Kevin Newman had wasted no time in arranging the destruction of the ancient cave that his former comrades had excavated. He stood in the middle of the dig site that he had once presided over as chief archaeologist. Today though, he was presiding over the disposal of contaminated water. Despite his annoyance with Anne, he was not looking forward to having a face-to-face confrontation with her.

He impatiently checked his watch as the maintenance crew lowered one end of a huge hose into the opening of the cave. He was anxious for them to start pumping fluid into the cave before Anne or any of her crew arrived on the scene. The maintenance crew did not share his sense of urgency and seemed to be taking an age to position their equipment. Finally, the worker who had dropped the hose into the cave looked up and gave his colleague the thumbs up. His colleague, wearing an apparently unnecessary protective helmet, began to turn the large faucet at the other end of the hose. The faucet was connected to a pipeline designed to bring chlorinated water into the as-yet-unbuilt swimming pool.

Dr. Pargiter, following the instructions of Newman, had diverted the contaminated water down the pipeline. The maintenance man controlling the faucet released his grip. The hosepipe started to expand as the blood-filled water raced towards the ancient cavern. Newman watched the bulge, marking the head of the water, edge down into the cavern. The sound of gushing liquid began to echo from beneath the ground. Newman was finally able to relax slightly. The archaeological crew had missed the opportunity to stop the disposal of the hazardous liquid.

However, his sense of relief was short-lived as a familiar voice captured his attention.
"You vandal," cried Anne as she burst through the chain-link gate that separated the dig site from the rest of the resort.
"I thought you were a complete sell-out but I didn't realize you were a complete sleaze bag." She raced towards him. Padraig, who had been unable to keep up with her during the sprint from the desalination plant, made his way through the gate gasping for breath.

In anticipation of her arrival, Newman had already made arrangements to take care of her. Two security guards armed with assault rifles came running over and positioned themselves between the angry archaeologist and her former boss.

"She is the one you've been looking for. Arrest her," ordered Newman.
One of the guards marched up to Anne, raised his gun to her chest, and used his weapon to gesture to the gate from which she had just entered.
"You've got to be kidding?" said Anne to Kevin. Newman ignored her and instead clicked his fingers. The other guard promptly marched over to the gate and held it open so his colleague could escort the prisoner to her cell. Much as she wanted to attack Newman both physically and verbally, Anne could sense that these guards were a little trigger happy. She didn't want to take a bullet for the sake of an already destroyed ancient artifact. She silently made her way through the gate accompanied by the guards.

Padraig meanwhile, had just about recaptured his breath and was amazed to see the whole scene unfold. Newman, suddenly had an uneasy look on his face as if he realized he was about to make front page news.
"Erm you may be wondering what's going on here," Newman said. He quickly tried to conjure up a believable sounding explanation for Anne's arrest and the flooding of the cave. Much to his relief, Padraig interrupted him and put his mind at ease. "It's OK. She is a nutter, probably involved with that other chap Beauchamp had banged up. The Liberian." Newman decided to accept Padraig's words at face value. "As long as we're on the same page then," replied Newman before nonchalantly exiting the dig site with a self-satisfied grin across his face.

Padraig glanced across at the maintenance guy standing over the cave entrance. The man stared back at him making Padraig feel as if he had outstayed his welcome. "Good work," said Padraig to the maintenance man who offered no response. Padraig regretted the fact that halfway to the dig site, his colleague Danny had decided to stop at security to pick up an extra memory card for his camera from his luggage. He had seen plenty of strange things during his brief time on the island but had very little photographic evidence to back any of it up.

As Padraig pondered his next move he realized the maintenance man was still staring at him wondering when he was going to leave. The journalist gave a half-hearted wave before turning and heading for the gate. Padraig pulled the chain link gate shut. As it clattered behind him, Danny suddenly appeared in the corridor in front of him.

Danny seemed to be just as out of breath as Padraig had been a few minutes earlier.
"You really need to start working out more Danny," said Padraig unsympathetically.
Danny winced as he caught his breath. "I just saw Anne," he said, "it looked like some guards were taking her to the security area."
"Yeah," said Padraig "things are starting to get a little bit out of control here. I am going to pick up our bags from security and find out where the heck our room is. I need to start writing some of this stuff into a nice little story. Should keep Claudia entertained for a day or two but I need you to take some photos."
"What do you need?" Asked Danny.
"Anything you can get," replied Padraig.
"I'll see what I can do."
"Good man," said Padraig. He gave his friend a hearty pat on the shoulder before heading off towards security. Danny wasted no time. Grabbing hold of the camera hanging around his neck, he snapped dozens of pictures of the waste disposal exercise going on behind the chain link fence.

Edith stood waiting patiently in the restaurant area for her tour group to return. It was 20 minutes after the rendezvous and not a tourist was in site. Just as she was about to start searching the complex, Mike Patel appeared at the top of the stairwell that led down into the restaurant. He also seemed surprised to find the restaurant empty. He raised his hands in bewilderment before slowly descending the staircase. Following close behind him was his wife Gita. As ever, she seemed intent to keep a low profile by staying in his shadow.

As the Patel's reached ground level, the sound of clattering feet began to echo throughout the otherwise silent dining area. The rest of the group appeared and noisily stomped their way down the stairwell. Edith was surprised to see that very few of the guests had actually changed into their swimwear. A few of the older women were wearing bathing suits that were concealed beneath dressing gowns. Mike Patel had switched out his casual slacks and dress-shirt for some more formal slacks and a crisper looking shirt. Most of the other men had followed suit. They had dressed as if they were heading to a dinner party rather than a swimming pool.

Billy Bradshaw was the exception to the rule. Everyone around him seemed uncomfortable at the sight of his snugly fitting brown Speedo. His girlfriend Sam and son Ben were wearing the same short and T-shirt combinations they had been wearing before they left.

The group congregated around Edith who greeted them with a warm smile.
"Well, I'm glad to see that several of you decided to put on your bathing suits because we have a really great area outside which has several slides and a fountain. I think you will have a lot of fun. Those of you who didn't change into your swimwear will be feeling very jealous." She giggled as she delivered her last sentence.

As she walked towards the glass patio doors, whispered squabbling broke out behind her as a few women berated their spouses for dressing inappropriately. Edith led the group through the automatic sliding glass doors out onto a vast patio featuring an hourglass-shaped pool. At the opposite end of the pool were two spiral-shaped, multi-colored slides. Guests could access the slides via a metallic staircase or a glass elevator. Either side of the pool were rows of sunbeds. Beyond the sunbeds were hot tubs and several larger swimming pools all of which were equipped with either slides or a wave machine.

The tour group began to dissipate and the curious travelers wandered around the pool. Ben ran off at high speed towards the stairwell leading to the slide on the right-hand side of the pool. Billy went sprinting after him. Mike Patel was less than impressed with the pool but the fountain in the center caught his attention. It consisted of a huge statue of the Roman god Neptune, who held a trident in one hand and a net in the other. Water was spraying out from the three points on the trident but a larger quantity of water was blasting upwards out of the middle of Neptune's head. It was an unusual spectacle, and he was curious enough to take a closer look.

Edith was pleased to see the group enjoying themselves even if none of them had yet ventured into the water. The sound of the automatic glass doors opening caused her to turn around. As she did, a flash from Danny's camera caused her to blink.
"Oh," she was startled "I didn't expect to see you there." Danny lowered his camera to his chest.
"Padraig needs me to take some pictures. There is a lot of crazy stuff going on here."
"Oh yes?" Edith was disconcerted "What kind of crazy stuff?"
"I will tell you later," said Danny as he raised his camera and began taking snaps of the pool area.

"Aarrgghh," a shrill scream shattered the calm ambiance around the pool. Everybody turned and looked in unison to see who had screamed. Gita Patel was standing with her hands over her face at the edge of the pool directly across from the fountain. Mike Patel who was standing close by, placed his right arm around her shoulder. She responded by turning and burying her face into his chest.

"What is the problem?" said Edith turning to Danny. He had already gone. The second he had heard a scream he had sprinted down the side of the pool. As everybody else began to make their way towards the Patel's, Danny, fully clothed, jumped into the pool. Even from several yards away he had seen something large floating in the water under the shadow of the fountain. As the rest of the group gathered behind him, he reached down into the water and gripped the shoulder of the body floating at his feet. With one decisive heave, he flipped the body over. There were horrified gasps as several of the guests recognized the dead man as being Hugh Pompidou.

Danny looked up irritated at the spectators and gestured for help. None was forthcoming until Billy emerged at the bottom of the nearby slide. The Londoner ran to Danny's aid. Together, the two men dragged the lifeless body to the edge of the pool. The onlookers instinctively moved back and left a space on the patio just large enough for them to lay out the corpse. Pompidou was dead but Danny felt compelled to try and revive him. He had no knowledge of first aid but he sank to his knees, put his hands together and started pounding on Pompidou's midriff. Several of the onlookers, realizing Pompidou was dead, turned away while morbid curiosity kept others engaged in the proceedings.

After a few seconds of chest pounding, Danny decided to put pressure on the old man's stomach instead. It had occurred to him that Pompidou had ingested water and perhaps could be revived. Danny placed his fist on the old man's stomach exerting as much pressure as he could muster. His efforts were to no avail but encouraged by his persistence, Billy decided to join in. He started pounding the other side of Pompidou's stomach. After almost a minute of clobbering the lifeless corpse, their efforts seemed to be rewarded as his chest lurched slightly upwards. Suddenly, an ice cube was propelled from the back of his throat onto the patio beside his head. Danny and Billy thought he was reviving. Unseen by them, a physician had now arrived on the scene.

Dr. Hewlett was the only doctor at Aqua Monde although the company had hired more than a dozen nurses to handle minor medical issues. Hewlett pushed Danny and Billy to one side. She was a heavyset woman in her 50s. She awkwardly knelt on the patio desperately hoping her skirt wouldn't split. She checked Pompidou's vital signs but it was apparent for all to see that her arrival had come too late. Without a word, she pulled his eyelids down over his lifeless eyeballs and clumsily rose to her feet. Danny and Billy expected her to commend them for their efforts. Instead, she pulled a walkie-talkie from her inside jacket pocket. Holding down the speaker button she gave a grim command, "get a body bag down here."

Edith, suddenly aware of her job duties, started to round up the distraught tourists.
She shepherded them back to the restaurant that they had been cooped up in for most of the day. Danny and Billy stayed behind with the doctor who was now instant messaging on her cellphone. Billy liked to be the center of attention. He wanted to be there when they took away the body he had helped to retrieve it.

Danny had encountered plenty of death and destruction during his career as a photographer. He was almost as unmoved about the old man's death as the doctor. He was though frustrated that he had not found the body a few minutes earlier since he felt he could have been the hero of the day. He was keen to impress Edith. He feared the doctor's reaction to his efforts would leave Edith thinking of him as an idiot who roughs up dead bodies. His slight sense of embarrassment was the reason he had stayed behind.

Looking down at the ground, Danny noticed the rapidly melting ice cube that had seemingly been lodged in Pompidou's throat. Were it not for that tiny block of frozen water Pompidou would be alive and Danny wouldn't be feeling like an idiot. He bent down to snatch the ice cube off the ground. "A flipping ice cube !" he roared angrily as he furiously flung the offending item into the empty swimming pool.

The glass doors of the restaurant opened once again as Edith returned followed by Beauchamp and two grim-looking security officers. The group promptly marched over to Pompidou's lifeless body. One guard was holding a folding stretcher, the other grasped a black body bag. Edith stopped a few yards short of the body. She averted her gaze to avoid staring directly at the lifeless old man. Beauchamp knelt down beside Pompidou. Looking up, he addressed

Hewlett. "So what happened to him?"
"He choked on an ice cube," said Billy before Hewlett had a chance to respond. She turned and glared at him before affirming the accuracy of his statement.

"That's impossible," said Edith with indignation as she turned to face the others.
Danny was puzzled. "It's true," he said "we managed to expel the ice cube from his throat. You were standing right there weren't you?"
"Yes," said Edith "but then I remembered, he specifically told me he didn't want ice in his drink. I got the drink for him. It was plain water. I got him the AM spring water with no ice in it."

Hewlett was ready to return to her quarters and resume work on her online dating profile. "Mr. Beauchamp," said the doctor, "I am the only medical professional here and in my opinion, this individual choked to death on an ice cube. Now if you're done with me I'm a rather busy woman." Beauchamp had an ashen look on his face as he rose to his feet.
"Actually Dr. Hewlett," he said "I'm afraid there has been another incident. I need to ask you to head over to security. We need you to take a look at one of the prisoners in a detention cell." Hewlett let out a loud sigh and rolled her eyes. She hadn't expected to be so busy before the island was technically open for business.
"Very well," she said, "hopefully, I can do more for the next patient than we could do for this man." With a smirk, she trotted through the sliding glass doors.

Edith watched her disappear into the building before turning to Beauchamp and attempting to plead her case. "Mr. Beauchamp, I understand that these people are telling you this gentleman choked on an ice cube but I am telling you I know for a fact that is impossible." Beauchamp had no reason to doubt the credibility of the Doctor or the other witnesses. To avoid creating a scene, he thought it best the humor obviously distraught Edith. "Young lady," he said reassuringly "I will be conducting a full investigation into this matter. If there is anything you'd like to add to that investigation you are welcome to fill out a witness report form. If you come to security once we have disposed of the... corpse... I'll give you a form to fill out." Edith could sense that Beauchamp was simply trying to be polite and had no real interest in what she had to say. "Just forget it," she burst into tears and ran off towards the restaurant. Danny raced after her.

"Right gentlemen," said Beauchamp " let's get him out of her." The security guard holding the body bag loosened his grip and it slowly unraveled towards the ground.

Padraig entered the room he and Danny had been assigned. The door was covered with a layer of bamboo sticks to tie in with the 'Tiki' theme. He opened the door and fumbled in the dark for a light switch. His search was fruitless, but the delayed response of a motion sensor caused the lights to turn on. "Aghhhh," he screamed as he realized the room was occupied. He hadn't expected company. As his initial sense of shock dissipated, he realized the other party in the room was a disturbingly life-like, six-armed, Polynesian style mannequin complete with grass skirt, and a coconut shell bra. "Aloha." He was unnerved once again as the mannequin greeted him. "I am Leilani. May I take your coat? If you get lucky at the casino, I have plenty of hands to hold your companion's coat." The statement was capped with a canned snigger. Padraig shook his head in disbelief. "If I get lucky," he said, "I am sure my luck will change once my 'companion' sees a freaky looking octopus woman lurking in my room."

Padraig set his laptop on the bed -- a coconut styled hemisphere that was ideal for anyone wanting to sleep in the fetal position. At six feet tall, Padraig was unlikely to fit his entire frame on the oddly shaped mattress.

It was time to finish his first, and he strongly suspected, last article as the entertainment correspondent for Knox Media Conglomerate. He hoped the story he had pieced together would earn him a more worthwhile posting elsewhere. On the other hand, if his bosses were still intent to act as mindless cheerleaders for Aqua Monde, writing this article might just earn him the sack.

He sat on the end of the small bed hunched over his laptop. Anxiously tapping his right heel on the floor. He waited for the spellcheck to finish making his rushed work look respectable. The room was fairly small. It had white tiled flooring and off-white plasticky looking walls decorated with framed black-and-white stills of Polynesian islanders, and overhead shots of volcanic islands. The room had one small window. It was round. Shaped to look like a porthole, it reminded Padraig of his uncomfortable night on the cargo ship. As his word processing software analyzed his article, his animatronic companion suddenly began to talk. "At Aqua Monde we pride ourselves on being environmentally friendly. You can save water by hanging your wet towels in my arms. That way the cleaners will know not to replace them."

Padraig was about to look for an 'off' switch on Leilani when his laptop made a loud ping sound. The spellcheck was complete. Padraig saved his work and exited the document. He clicked on the toolbar to open up his e-mail session. He selected Claudia's name from his directory and attached the freshly finished work to an email. He didn't add a message to the story he had just composed. He felt that the article could do all of the talking.

He sat for a second wondering how she would react to the sensational story. Anxiety kicked in as he started to wonder if she would even read it since he hadn't included a cover message. Perhaps, she would think he had sent a blank email by mistake and delete it without even reading it. He wondered if he should send another email. She might get annoyed if she received the first e-mail and read it, only to receive a second email. That would imply he thought she lacked the intelligence to understand the purpose of the first email. He had screwed things up. "Blast," he said as he angrily slammed his laptop shut.

He would have to call her. He pulled his cell phone from his pocket; there was no reception. He noticed the phone sitting on top of the side table between the twin beds. Calls from hotels in the mainland United States were expensive enough so he could not imagine how much it would cost to make a call from here. Given everything else that was going on, running up a phone tab was the least of his worries. He placed his laptop on the bed and picked up the phone receiver. At first, he forgot to enter the international code for the US and the phone line responded by making a shrill whistling sound in his ear. He tried again, this time entering the number correctly.

It worked. The line was ringing. It kept ringing, he wondered if there was no answer because of the time difference. Looking at his watch he saw that it was 6 PM local time which meant it was 3 PM back in Florida. That was the time of day middle management could normally be found sipping obscenely large cappuccinos and surreptitiously reading horoscopes online.

"Thank you for calling Knox media conglomerates, this is Claudia Navarre, how can I be of assistance today?" the familiar but stern voice was suddenly on the other end of the line. "Claudia," he said, "it's Padraig."
"Padraig," she said crossly, "I thought we had lost you at sea or something. What the heck has been going on over there? I haven't heard from you or your buddy for two days."
"Well you are not going to believe the things that are going on here," whispered Padraig excitedly. He kept a nervous eye on the door, wondering if anyone was eavesdropping.
"What do you mean?" Asked Claudia suspiciously.
"I just sent you an email," he said. "we are talking big-time corporate corruption, fraud, ripping off Third World countries, destroying World Heritage sites. This place is nuts."
Padraig was giddy with excitement, this was the biggest exposé he had written in years.

"Let me stop you right there," replied Claudia firmly. Padraig's heart sank, he knew what was coming next. "We did not send you there to cause trouble. Do you understand what an entertainment reporter does?" Padraig was crestfallen. He knew Claudia was a career woman but hoped she had enough journalistic integrity to recognize an opportunity to promote some first-class investigative work.
"To be honest," he said sadly "I don't have the foggiest what an entertainment reporter does because I am not an entertainment reporter. I am a journalist and I am sorry that you seem to have forgotten that."

There was a long silence on the other end of the line. Claudia hadn't been expecting Padraig's remarks. It took her a moment to regain her composure and formulate a response. "You can either do the job we sent you to do or you can pick up your pink slip and get their hell out of there." She wasn't pulling any punches.
"You know what?" replied Padraig without hesitating "you can shove your job. I am a member of the Associated Press and I can sell my story to anyone I choose."

"And do you think anyone is going to believe you?" Claudia scoffed "a washed-up second-rate writer sending Bolshi emails from a water park in the middle of nowhere?"

"Yes," he replied calmly, "I think they will."

He placed the phone back onto the receiver. Things had been pretty ropey thus far. If she told the powers-that-be that he and Danny were no longer active reporters they would find themselves reduced to the status of stowaways. They had already sampled that role and it wasn't something he was keen to repeat. If he hung around, sooner or later someone would come knocking on his door and escort him off the island. There was only one thing they could do, go undercover.

FEAR

Flomo was sitting staring at the desk wondering how Padraig was getting along. Suddenly he was disturbed by the clanking of metal as someone on the other side of the door unfastened the bolt that was keeping him imprisoned. He was fearful that the guards were returning to rough him up some more. As the door swung open, he was surprised to see an unfamiliar face.

"Oh dear, that is a nasty gash," said Dr. Hewlett. She sauntered into the room followed by the guards who had administered the beating. They stared at Flomo menacingly from over her shoulder. Flomo gave her no more than a fleeting glance before staring down at the tabletop as he had been doing for the last few hours. Unperturbed, the Doctor approached him and began gently prodding the deep gash across his forehead. Flomo winced as she carelessly applied too much pressure to a particularly tender part of his wound. She ignored his apparent discomfort but after peering at his wounds she turned to look at the guards. She noticed how both men were staring at the prisoner with contemptuous looks.

" What the hell has been going on here?" She demanded. Flomo looked up and stared directly at the guards but neither man spoke. "You need to get one of the orderlies from sickbay to come down here and take care of this wound. He doesn't need a doctor, yet, but he will if you leave this wound to fester," she said.

Beauchamp, having overheard the commotion, decided to make an appearance. He had been told that Flomo had slipped and bumped his head, but he had not as of yet seen the injury. As he stood in the doorway, he gasped at the site of a six-inch gash that covered the best part of the Liberian's forehead. He had seen far worse wounds during his years in the military but he was mortified by the realization that his guards had lied to him. People don't bump their heads and slice half the skin off their foreheads.

Hewlett could see the shock on his face "Yes, horrible, isn't it? What kind of operation are you running here? This is supposed to be a vacation resort, not a banana republic!" Beauchamp was for once speechless. "How many other people have you locked up? I want to see them," demanded Hewlett " I am a doctor and anyone you detain has a right to medical access. I am that medical access."
"Yes," said the embarrassed Beauchamp " without delay. Right, this way."

He stepped back from the door and waited for Hewlett to follow him out into the hallway. Before she left, she gave Flomo a parting glance. It wasn't a friendly or sympathetic glance but it was intended to let him know that she was a professional and she was determined to do her job even if that meant ruffling some feathers along the way.

The guards followed her into the hallway and bolted the cell door closed. Beauchamp pulled back the huge metal bolt sealing the door on the opposite side of the hallway. Hewlett glanced inside the cell to see Anne sitting at a desk identical to the one in Flomo's cell. Anne looked up hopefully but Hewlett was silent. Satisfied that Anne had no external injuries she decided not to venture further. She stepped back into the hallway. Beauchamp firmly shut the door behind her.

"Anyone else?" asked the doctor. Beauchamp nodded before leading her further down the hallway to another bolted door. He slid back the stiff bolt and allowed the heavy door to swing open. Hewlett could not see anyone from the doorway as the entrance was located to the far left of one wall. She stepped inside, turned to the right and put her hands to her face as she gasped in horror. Seeing her reaction, from his position in the hallway, Beauchamp feared the worst. He rushed into the cell. For the second time in as many minutes, he found himself incapable of speech.

Henrik's lifeless body was sprawled across the floor, surrounded by a pool of blood. His skin was deathly white as if every blood cell had been drained from his body. His limbs looked brittle and stiff, his eyeballs had sunken back into his head. He had no visible entry wounds. Whatever the cause of his demise, it appeared as if he had been dead for some time. Hewlett, who had finally regained her composure, turned and left the room without a word. Beauchamp followed close behind.

The Security Chief was horrified. He had quickly come to the conclusion that his own guards had brutalized Flomo. While he believed them capable of viciousness, this was something else. Surely none of his hand-picked security officers would callously kill a defenseless detainee. Beauchamp knew he would have to investigate this matter himself before word got back to Jim Boyle. His job would be on the line regardless, but at least he would have a fighting chance if he could check the facts before this story came to light.

However, the time for Beauchamp to formulate a plan was already over. Jim Boyle was standing in the hallway waiting for him. Boyle was due to meet with the Security Chief that evening but he had decided to show up for an early meeting after hearing about the mysterious death of Mr. Pompidou. Technically, a choking death was not a security matter. Given the prior incident involving the water contamination, Boyle was on edge. He expected Beauchamp and his team to make sure nothing else went wrong.

"Beauchamp," said Boyle "what the hell happened? One of our guests was allowed to choke to death in the swimming pool and none of your goons even noticed."
"You've got more than that to worry about," said Hewlett.
"What are you talking about?" said Boyle, fearing the worst. Beauchamp sheepishly looked downwards while Hewlett gestured towards Henrik's cell. Boyle shoved past his Security Chief and stormed into the cell. He stood dumbfounded for a second before storming back out, raising his hands to Beauchamp's throat and pushing the old man against the wall.

"What the hell are you trying to do? You are going to get us all fired!" he yelled. His face was red with anger. He put his nose to Beauchamp's as he repeated both his question and statement while sending a splatter of phlegm all across Beauchamp's face. The guards who had been so willing to dole out violence themselves earlier in the day felt uneasy at seeing his physical aggressiveness towards their boss. Each guard grabbed one of Boyle's shoulders and pulled him clear of the Security Chief.

"You're fired! You're fired !" said Boyle angrily as he pointed an accusatory finger in Beauchamp's direction. He had never lost his composure to such an extent before but he had never been under such a public microscope The grand opening of the most expensive resort in the world was hours away and he was having to contend with a contaminated water supply, a belligerent group of archaeologists, and now two unexplained deaths. Boyle glared at everyone around him. Having already lost his cool he felt no need to try and adopt a sense of professionalism in the presence of these people.

"I am surrounded by idiots! Idiots!" he cried. He was close to breaking but he managed to compose himself enough to rattle off some instructions. "You two," he said to the guards "get him off this island." The "him" in question was a stunned Beauchamp. "There is a ship heading back to Monrovia overnight," Boyle continued "I want everyone on it who is a pain in the ass. The archaeologist girl, the rest of her group, these dead bodies, the terrorist, and anyone else who is not paid to be here or paying to be here." The security guards gave a nod to silently acknowledge his instructions. As Boyle departed from the security area, a sad looking Beauchamp looked across at the guards.

"It appears as though my work here is done, gentlemen. Just give me 20 minutes to gather my personal effects from my room. I will be back here so you can escort me to the ship." The guards were so used to taking orders from Beauchamp that they allowed him to depart unimpeded.

Beauchamp, had no intention of returning. He found himself in the unusual position of being a rule breaker rather than an enforcer. Given the prevailing circumstances, he felt that his services were still required on the islands, even if nobody had yet realized that. He reached the end of the corridor, slid his ID card through the reader on the wall and made his way through the sliding glass doors.

Despite his requests to have a room in close proximity to the security area, he had been assigned a room at the far end of the staff accommodation zone. The staff rooms were split across four levels. His room was at the far end of level three. He made his way up the stairs towards the second floor. There was an elevator, but he feared his former reports would regret the decision to let him wander freely around the complex, and would come after him. Taking the stairs would make it easier for him to avoid detection.

As he reached the top of the staircase, swing glass doors that divided it from the next level swung open. Padraig came bursting through clattering into the old man in the process. Beauchamp fell to his knees as a result of the impact. Padraig, red-faced and breathless, resisted the urge to keep moving and helped the man -- he feared was on his way to arrest him -- get back to his feet.
Beauchamp, obviously shaken, attempted to downplay the incident as Padraig offered a series of half-hearted apologies.
"No damage done," said Beauchamp "in fact our little meeting is quite fortuitous as you are just the man I needed to see."

Padraig's heart sank. He had hoped it would have taken longer for word to get to Beauchamp that he was no longer on the islands as an active reporter. "That didn't take long," said Padraig.
"No," said Beauchamp sadly "the loss of a job is a strange thing."
"Strange indeed," said Padraig, who had no idea Beauchamp was talking about his own lack of employment. "But I rather think you might be able to help me," said Beauchamp quietly "with your influence on the powers-that-be, you may be able to rectify my little problem."

Padraig was confused "I'm sorry? You want me to help you?" Beauchamp, blissfully ignorant of Padraig's own situation, had been hoping for a more positive response. "Well, I'm sorry if I misread the situation. I rather thought that my cooperation with your interrogation of the prisoner was worthy of at least a quiet word in someone's ear. I suppose a 40-year career of distinguished service means nothing to a young man like you."

Padraig suddenly realized that the two men were talking about entirely different things. By the sound of it, Beauchamp's own job was somehow in jeopardy.
"You lost your job?" he asked.
Beauchamp, still shocked at the whole situation, said nothing but his stern stare told Padraig everything he needed to know. "What happened?" asked the journalist.
"It is all rather odd. Those guards, the men I hired . . . I knew, some of them were blaggards, roughnecks, whatever you want to call them. I saw that myself when I was working for a security firm in Liberia. Some of these men were contractors working for me… But I never thought them capable of murder!"
"Murder?"
"Well, murder seems the most likely explanation. Poor young man, Norwegian or something. One of those archaeologists, dead in his cell. Blood everywhere."
Padraig's thoughts drifted to an archaeologist he knew rather better. "What about Anne? Where is she? Did they do anything to her?" Padraig was visibly agitated and concerned for the young woman's safety. Beauchamp was quick to reassure him. "No, She's fine. They are shipping her out on a boat tonight. Well, her, me, the rest of her crew, the terrorist chap - who incidentally someone took a rifle butt to the face."

The hissing sound of the announcement system coming to life suddenly caught their attention. A nervous sounding male voice, obviously unfamiliar with public speaking, began to talk. "This is a security announcement. The following staff members and miscellaneous personnel need to report to the cargo area in the desalination plant within the hour: Robert Beauchamp, Kenny Tsang, Terrance James, Padraig Coyle, and Danny Clifton. Please bring all your belongings with you."
"You?" said Beauchamp.
"Yes," said Padraig "you're not the only one who lost your job

today. Anyway, I don't know about you but I have no intention of getting on that boat." Beauchamp stretched his right hand towards Padraig. The journalist reciprocated and gave the man a hearty handshake.
"Very good," said Beauchamp "so what is the plan?"

Terrance and Kenny had already been told to pack their bags by Kevin Newman. They were patiently waiting at the dock by the desalination plant as the tannoy announcement went out. A simple chain, 4 feet above the ground sealed off the gangplank that led from the dock to the ship. No sooner had the announcement finished then a burly looking Nigerian crewmember appeared on deck and made his way down the gangplank. He unclipped one end of the chain and gestured for the two scientists to come aboard. It was the same boat they had arrived on just hours earlier.

"Hold up," said a voice from further down the dock. The two men turned to see a somber procession heading their way. Two security guards were pushing a two-tier metal cart with what appeared to be an occupied body bag on each level. The cart came trundling past Kenny and Terrance as the two guards rolled it across the gangplank onto the boat.

"Looks like you've got some real stiffs on your boat," said a voice from behind the scientists. Kenny turned around to see investment officer Owen Gaunt standing before him, with a cigarette in one hand and a glass of scotch in the other. Owen shook his head sadly as the guards pushing the cart disappeared into the boat.
"That Mr. Pompidou would have been a good client. But all the bonds in the world can't help the poor old coot now." Gaunt raised his glass in the air to toast Pompidou.
After a second of silent contemplation, Gaunt turned his attention to Kenny.

"Well you are a long way from home aren't you?" he said.
"What is that supposed to mean?" Terrance demanded.
"Simply that he is the first Chinese I have seen on the island. I expect we will see plenty more of you guys. You've got all that money from the Federal government bonds, as well as the profits from all the plastic crap you guys sell through our big box retail stores." Gaunt smiled and stood waiting for some kind of humorous retort from Kenny. Instead, the archaeologist had a puzzled look.
"You know that I am from Scotland right?" he said, "and you realize that you are perpetuating offensive racial stereotypes."

"Hey if we're at the point where we can't have little banter then political correctness has obviously gone too far."

Gaunt took a deep draw on his cigarette causing the orange glow to expand towards his fingers. Pulling the cigarette away from his mouth, he let out a forceful blast of smoke in the direction of Terrance. Waving his hands in the air to drive away the smoke Terrance turned away and began to cough.
"You know that smoking is going to kill you right?" Said Kenny.
"If I had a dollar for everything I have been told was going to kill me during my life I'd have over $50 by now," quipped Gaunt. He chuckled, amused at his own joke and flung his half-spent cigarette into the sea below.

"Have either of you gentlemen seen Bob Beauchamp? Kind of an old guy? He runs security here." Terrance didn't respond as he was too busy sniffing the inside of his T-shirt. He was trying to establish if the residual smell of smoke was bad enough to warrant changing his outfit. Kenny responded with a shrug of his shoulders. "Well if you see him, tell him that Owen Gaunt said 'Bon Voyage,'" blurted Gaunt, before downing the remainder of his scotch. "Back to work," he said to himself as he lit up another cigarette and strolled back towards the resort area. "You know that guy is the top investment rep trying to get people to invest in the resort right?" said Kenny. "Yeah, I remember him from that orientation seminar we went to. No wonder sales are down. Part Mad Men, part George Wallace." said Terrance.

The guards who had taken the bodies on board finally emerged from the bowels of the ship. They marched past the archaeologists on the dockside. The Nigerian crewmember reappeared and gestured for Terrance and Kenny to come aboard. They each grabbed their bags and made their way across the noisy metal gangplank.

"Hey I wonder who's in the body bags," said Kenny.
"Didn't he say it was one of his investment clients?" Said Terrance.
"Yeah, ONE of his investment clients but there are two body bags. I wonder who is in the other one."
" No one significant," said Terrance "otherwise we would have had

all the important people down here for the send-off."

"True," said Kenny "but it's kind of freaky having two dead bodies on board don't you think?"

"I'd rather have two dead people than two jackasses like those journalists who were on the boat coming over," replied Terrance. Kenny wasn't so sure.

Still brooding about the lack of interest Anne had shown in him, Terrance was glad to leave the island. Kenny would have preferred to stay but as ever he was trying to remain in a positive mood. They made their way to the small metal cabin they had shared on the journey over. Terrance dropped his bag on the floor and collapsed face down on the bottom bunk. Kenny laughed "Man you've got it bad."

Kenny knew they would have plenty of time to sleep in the coming hours so he wasn't eager to confine himself to his bunk just yet. "So what are we going to do when we get to Liberia?" asked Kenny excitedly. "Get on a plane and go home," mumbled Terrance with his face firmly embedded in his pillow. "We have 12 hours before our flight," said Kenny "don't you want to explore the city a bit?" Terrance murmured something indistinguishable to which Kenny just laughed.

"Hey, I wonder what happened to Henrik?" said Kenny who was unable to keep his thoughts to himself. Terrance shrugged his shoulders disinterestedly without looking up.

"Well I mean they didn't even call his name out. Do you think Kevin is letting him stay here to do some work." Terrance finally sat on his bed.

"No," said Terrance, "he told me that if anyone was going to stay here it would be me because I'm the best scientist in our group." Terrance made his statement with such forcefulness that Kenny didn't want to argue, despite viewing Terrance as the weak link in the team.

Despite his self-confidence, Terrance was perturbed that Henrik's name had not been read out. Perhaps Kevin had lied to him and maybe Henrik had been given some other kind of role. "That ain't right, "said Terrance "if he did let him stay. He told me I was the only one with any credibility. The rest of you got pushed around by Anne too much."

Kenny wanted to argue but his roommate was in a dark mood that from Kenny's perspective was quite intimidating.

The sound of footsteps dragging along the metal hallway caught Kenny's attention

Eager to focus on anything other than Terrance's sulking he turned to look down the corridor. A tall, thin figure was making its way towards their room. In the dimly lit ship, it was difficult to make out anything other than the basic outline of a man. Kenny wondered who it might be. Perhaps the journalist. He hoped not, as he already had one miserable roommate to contend with.

The dark figure slowly trudged his way towards the room before finally catching the light. He stopped inches short of the oval-shaped doorway. Kenny was pleased to see a familiar face. "Henrik! Where have you been, man? I have been stuck here with this miserable git." Henrik did not respond. He stared vacantly at Kenny. His face, which was always gaunt, seemed somehow paler than normal. " What's the matter?" asked Kenny "you know Henrik you're not looking so good are you feeling okay?"

Henrik smirked.

Danny was making his way towards the dock area. He had no luggage. Having returned to his room, he discovered both his colleagues' and his belongings had gone AWOL. He had no idea where Padraig could have gone. Having run out of things to take pictures of he had been loitering around the restaurant area while Edith was doing her best to keep the increasingly unhappy visitors entertained. She seemed to genuinely like him but circumstances had conspired against him. It is never easy to win the heart of a girl when you have showers of blood and dead corpses to contend with, thought Danny.

He was not particularly unhappy to hear the announcement telling him to leave the island. He was slightly mystified as to the reasons, but he assumed Padraig must've done something to upset someone. That was usually the case when the two men were asked to leave places. Danny wandered past the corridor leading to the security area and turned left down the long hallway that led directly to the desalination plant. Maybe Padraig was waiting for him on the boat.

Danny was startled as a hand appeared from a closet to his right and gripped his arm. As the door of the closet opened a few inches more, he was able to see that the head on the shoulders at the end of the arm belonged to Padraig. He put the forefinger of his other hand to his lip as a signal for Danny to remain silent. He let go of his friend's arm and stepped back into the closet, signaling for Danny to join him inside.

Danny hesitated for a moment wondering if it would be better to leave Padraig to his own devices. The ship was past the glass door at the end of the hallway. No more than 50 yards from where Danny stood. He could be back home within a few days, watching soccer, having a beer and not having to worry about any of this drama anymore. Despite his desire for the simple life, his sense of loyalty persuaded him to follow his friend into the small looking closet.

Checking to see that no one else was around, Danny crept inside. It was pitch black and cramped. Danny could feel a box pushed up against his right leg, and what felt like mop handles were poking into his rib cage. Somewhere in the closet, unseen was Padraig.

"Well what the hell is going on?" demanded Danny in a loud voice. Padraig responded with a loud "shhh" that sent a spray of saliva in Danny's direction.
"You're sure we can trust him?" said a deep voice that wasn't Padraig's.
"Who else is in here with us?" said, Danny doing his best to whisper.
"Beauchamp," said Padraig in a barely audible voice.
"What the heck is he doing here?" said Danny, forgetting to whisper. Padraig launched another loud "Shssh" and an accompanying spray of salvia at his friend. Enough droplets of moisture landed on Danny's face this time to ensure he would not forget to whisper again. "He is helping us," explained Padraig "one of Anne's team got killed by the guards…we think."
"Killed?" exclaimed Danny.
"Yes, murdered… by someone…it would appear," Padraig continued, "they sacked Beauchamp and want to get him, us, Anne and her crew as well as Flomo, off the island before the grand opening tomorrow. We plan to stay here and find out what is really going on."
"I see," said Danny "but don't you think they are going to notice that we are not on the ship?"
"Obviously!" Said Padraig "which is why we are hiding in this closet."
" So we plan to stay here in his cramped dark uncomfortable broom cupboard until the ship leaves the dock several hours from now."
"Precisely," replied Padraig.
Danny rolled his eyes but no one was able to see him. The urge to open the door and make a dash for freedom was stronger than ever. Somehow he found himself reluctantly agreeing to the ridiculous sounding plan.

Anne's cell door opened and a guard clutching an assault rifle appeared in the doorway. He instructed Anne to make her way into the corridor. It was time for her to leave Aqua Monde. She was surprised to see her luggage holdall stuffed to the brim sitting on the floor outside her cell. The guard gestured for her to pick it up. With a sneer, she bent down, grabbed the holdall and flung it forcefully over her shoulder so as to 'accidentally' hit the guard in the face.

The guard didn't react. He had already allowed his violent streak to rear its head earlier in the day. The man on the receiving end of it was standing in the hallway just a few yards from Anne. Unlike his fellow prisoner, Flomo's hands were tied with plastic cuffs. Another guard was holding an assault rifle and was keeping a careful eye on the Liberian.

"So what does a janitor do to end up in handcuffs?" Anne asked of Flomo.
"I got involved in a little water pollution. How about you?" He replied.
"I got in a little argument about dumping your handiwork in a cave containing priceless artifacts." A prod in the back with the end of the rifle signaled to Flomo that the time for exchanging stories was over. With one guard in front and one behind, Anne and Flomo were marched down the hallway towards the desalination plant.

As they approached the glass doors that led out onto the dock Anne thought she saw a pair of eyes peering out from a barely open closet door. Someone was hiding from the guards she assumed. Anne was a great believer in the old adage that "my enemy's enemy is my friend." Consequently, she decided it best to ignore the concealed individual for fear of drawing attention to someone potentially battling the same corporation as her.

The quartet reached the glass doors that obligingly slid open. They made their way out onto the dockside. As they approached the boat they could hear that a furious argument was underway. The people arguing were out of sight. As they reached the gangplank leading to the boat they could see a group of Nigerian crewmembers furiously remonstrating with the captain of the ship.

Just visible beyond the arguing crew members was Kevin Newman who was watching with interest from outside the crew cabins. Two of the crew members were taking it in turns to violently prod the captain's chest while launching phlegmatic tirades in his direction. The captain was remaining surprisingly calm. Newman, clearly unable to understand what was being discussed, had his eyes fixed upon the captain who would occasionally turn to him and mumble an abbreviated translation of what had been said.

The new arrivals stood silently on the other side of the gangplank feeling awkward and out of place. The two guards had been given strict instructions to frog march the prisoners to the ship. Neither man felt inclined to try and barge past the angry scene unfolding before them. Anne noticed that Flomo had his head tilted sideways and was seemingly straining to hear what was being said.
"What are they saying?" She asked.
"They are arguing."
"I can see that," she said with exasperation "what are they arguing about?"
"I don't know," he said, "I think they are talking in Yoruba or Igbo, West African dialects I am not that familiar with. I had a friend from Nigeria and I would hear him on the phone with his family. While the language sounds familiar, the words mean nothing to me."

The two men who had been leading the remonstrating seemed to have finished arguing their case. After a moment of silence and a brief exchange of glances with the rest of the crew, the two turned and made their way down the gangplank onto the deck. Their less vocal colleagues quickly followed them leaving a frustrated looking captain with his hands on his hips. The Nigerians made their way past the small group of onlookers and went through the glass doors that led to the main resort.

Kevin Newman took a step onto the deck. He had a horrified look on his face as he saw the men disappear into the building. Once they were out of sight he turned and raised an accusatory finger in the

direction of the captain. "Where have they gone?" he demanded to know. "They are very superstitious," offered the captain, "they think this boat is cursed. They do not want to travel on it until it has been exorcised."
"You need to get them back here right now and tell them that if they don't get back on the boat they are guilty of mutiny." Newman delivered his statement forcefully but the captain, twice his width and the least a foot taller than him, was not impressed. He chuckled, placed a hand on Newman's shoulder and said: "you tell them." He then exited down the gangplank and hurried after his crew.

Newman was dumbfounded. He was a scientist who had suddenly found his job duties increased to include security. It was all due to the firing of Beauchamp, and Boyle's complete lack of faith in any of the security guards. "How's the new job working out for you?" scoffed Anne. An embarrassed Newman did his best to pretend he had not heard her remark.

The ever-busy sliding glass doors opened once again, this time to reveal the shapeless figure of Dr. Hewlett. She had a face like thunder as she stomped her way towards Newman. She was barely within earshot of them when she began to yell in his direction. "You know that I'm supposed to be off work right now?" She said "you also know that when I took this job I signed on to be a doctor, not a mortician?" she neither expected a response nor waited for one. Instead, she deliberately knocked Newman aside with a flailing elbow. She made her way onto the ship and down the long barely lit hallway that led to the crew's quarters.

Newman was in no hurry to follow her given her mood but he felt equally uncomfortable hanging around in close proximity to his former protégé, Anne. After a few moments of silent reflection he decided to follow the doctor and made his way towards the end of the hallway.
All the doors onboard were shut except one. It led into the room Kenny and Terrance had claimed as their own just an hour earlier. Dr. Hewlett was in there making a racket. Newman could hear her shuffling things around, talking to herself about employees rights, and how she wished she had a quiet country practice. She was an

intimidating figure when she was angry. Newman, in his new-found role as Security Chief, had no option but to ask for her assessment of the bloody scene in the cabin.

He silently stepped in through the oval-shaped doorway and cast his eyes onto the horrific scene inside the room. Sitting against the wall to his right was the lifeless body of Kenny Tsang. His head was bent down against his chest. A triangular stain of blood stretched out from a narrow point on his neck all the way down to his waist. A Frisbee sized pool of blood was congealing on the floor to Kenny's left.

Hewlett meanwhile, was kneeling down over Terrance's corpse. He was face down on the floor in a pool of blood. A fist-sized patch of flesh and clothing was missing from the center of his back. His shirt seemed to have sunken into his body. Torn pieces of blood-soaked fabric were indistinguishable from his innards. Judging by the scar, something sizable had been used to stab or even impale him thought Kevin. Hewlett had been casting her eye over the wound. She was looking for a fragment of wood, metal or anything else that might have become detached from the weapon used to slay the scientist. She found nothing. Clearly, whatever it was, a different and much smaller weapon had been used to kill Kenny.

"Well?" asked Newman.
Hewlett awkwardly got onto her feet. "Well," she said "I'm not a forensic scientist but if I was to make a guess I would say that someone stabbed that guy in the throat. This guy ... I have no idea! Looking at his back you think someone had driven a stake through him. Whoever did this is a very violent and a dangerous individual and this is something we really need to turn over to the FBI."
"We can't do that," said Newman.
"Jurisdiction?" asked Hewlett.
" No. Shareholders. We have the grand opening tomorrow morning. We cannot have the opening day of the biggest and most expensive water resort in the world overshadowed by some kind of Jack the Ripper wannabe. We must keep this under wraps for at least a couple of days."

Hewlett was appalled at what he was suggesting. "You know that

just because you create your own patch of land in the middle of the ocean doesn't mean you can live without ethics," she said.
" Don't talk to me about ethics. I spent a whole career worrying about ethics and where did it get me?"

With a loud beep, the walkie-talkie hanging from Newman's belt came to life. He picked it up and held it to his mouth. "Newman," he said.
"So Furman tells me we have a mutiny on our hands," said the crackly voice on the end of the walkie-talkie. It was Boyle, a man who had seemed on the verge of a nervous breakdown last time Newman had seen him. "What do you want me to do?" asked Newman. "I want that girl of yours and that terrorist and the rest of the misfits off the island. Since we can't find anyone capable of manning the ship, you'll have to send them back using your own boat."

Newman did not like that suggestion. As a perk of his job, he had been given a two deck high-speed yacht. He'd been planning on trying to find some female company to take on an impromptu champagne cruise on the night of the grand opening. However, Boyle didn't sound as if he was in the mood for negotiations. "OK," said Newman meekly "what about the bodies?"
"Keep them here. At some point, we are going to have to have a proper investigation but we need to keep that on ice for a while. Get them over to the desalination plant. Pargiter has some industrial sized freezers there where we can keep them for the time being." With another beep and a loud crackle, the walkie-talkie went dead. "Well you can move them yourself, " snapped Hewlett.

Newman was for the first time starting to wonder if he had made a terrible decision when he decided to trade in his tweed jacket for a life on the high seas. Hewlett went trudging off down the hallway. After a second of hesitation, Newman put his anxiety to one side and went marching after her. He caught up with the belligerent doctor as she exited the boat.

As he was about to speak, he realized that Anne and Flomo were still standing on the dock. He wasn't particularly keen to get into a discussion about the slaughter of Kenny and Terrance in front of their former work colleague. He allowed Hewlett to waddle off as he turned his attention to the wayward archaeologist, and the Liberian who had unknowingly given him the ammunition he needed, to destroy Anne's amazing find.

"Take these two down to my boat," Newman instructed the nearest guard. "The cabin's are in a mess… I was entertaining last night you see… So anyway stick them on deck for the time being until we get ahold of the captain." The guard used his gun to point Flomo and Anne in the direction of the boat.
"So we are getting an upgrade?" Asked Anne sarcastically.
"Something like that," snapped Newman.
"Well, what happened to the others?" Demanded Anne.
"The others are not coming with you," said Newman "they are going to stay here."
"Five minutes ago their names were being read out and the guy on the tannoy certainly seemed to think they would be coming with us. As did whoever dropped their bags off down the hallway."

As Anne finished her sentence she lent over the gangplank and pointed towards the crew cabins on the boat. The dead scientists' bags were resting up against the door behind which they had been murdered. Newman pursed his lips for a second as he tried to think of a suitable manner in which to lie his way out of this situation. However, given that it was going to take a couple of days for his boat to get to shore, he realized that the news of the duo's death was likely to break long before Anne reached Liberia. Therefore, he may as well tell her the truth.

"They are dead."
"What do you mean 'they are dead?'" Anne demanded.
"Someone killed them. I don't know who. I don't know how. If you two had been here about 10 minutes earlier then you would probably be dead too. OK, no more questions. Get them out of here."

Newman clicked his fingers above his head and then walked off towards the main building without giving Anne or the others a second glance. She started walking towards him but was quickly stopped by one of the guards who blocked her with his rifle. Having seen what happened to Flomo, she decided not to argue. She turned and started to make her way down the dockside. Flomo silently walked beside her. After a few minutes, the duo and the guards that were accompanying them arrived at a two-level yacht which was gently bouncing around in the increasingly choppy water.

One guard remained on the dockside as his colleague escorted the prisoners to the captain's deck which was on the second floor. The escort locked the door behind him and scurried down the stairwell to join his colleague on the dockside. Since Newman and Hewlett had cleared the area, nobody else was around. After a brief exchange of raised eyebrows and shoulder shrugs, the two guards decided it was an opportune moment to have a surreptitious smoke.

After about 30 seconds of calmness, their smoke break was interrupted by the sound of an engine starting up. Both men reacted with irritation as the noisy motor reverberated around the narrow dock area. It was already too late for them to do anything when they realized that the engine in question was located on the boat in front of them. To their amazement, the yacht abruptly broke away from the shoreline causing the attached gangplank to fall into the water. If they had reacted more quickly they could have jumped aboard but the boat was already racing away from the shore.

Onboard, Flomo peered nervously out of the front window, half expecting to see a fleet of security vessels waiting to intercept them. However, beyond the ship they had been originally intending to travel on, there were no other boats to be seen. Flomo turned to his left where Anne was watching over his shoulder. "What a prat that guy is," chuckled Flomo "if you are going to imprison people you should not leave knives lying around if you use plastic handcuffs."
"How is it you know how to drive one of these things anyway?" Asked Anne.
"I used to be a stockbroker in London," replied Flomo cheerfully.
"So you have ridden on yachts before?"
"Ridden?" Laughed Flomo "until the 2008 crash I owned a bunch of these things."

REVELATIONS

Claudia's horoscope didn't look too promising she thought. "Thunderstorms darken your horizon this week," it said. She tried to interpret its meaning. Claudia couldn't help but think it had something to do with Padraig although he had been darkening the skies in her world for many months now. She moved her cursor over the x-mark in the top left-hand corner of the horoscope webpage. With a quick tap of a finger, the gloomy prediction was gone.

The only other open tab on her monitor was the Knox media conglomerate news page. In the center of the screen was a tiny video window in which a female reporter was gesticulating wildly as she reported on a seemingly important event. Claudia shuffled her mouse and dragged the cursor over the volume control so that she could hear what the reporter was saying.

"The sense of excitement is rapidly building here at Aqua Monde as the celebrity guests continue to arrive." Claudia rolled her eyes. She should have known better than to turn on the news today of all old days. The whole world was waiting to hear about the grand opening of the biggest man-made structure in the world. She was having to deal with the petty tantrums of the one reporter who didn't want to be there. Despite her sense of frustration, a kind of morbid curiosity drove her to expand the video window so she could get a better view of the event.
"The organizers here tell me that all of the preparations have gone off without a hitch," said the blonde headed, fair skinned reporter. "Normally, they tell me, you would expect to have some kind of technical problems at an event of this magnitude. But so far the sun is shining, the crowds are cheering and this is the one resort in the world where everyone wants to be." Even accounting for the sycophantic reporters' obvious bias thought Claudia, it was

impossible to reconcile this newscast with the hysterical version of events she had heard from Padraig. "I'll kill him when he gets back," Claudia yelled at her PC screen. "Now if you look behind me," continued the reporter as if she were directly talking to Claudia "you can see some of the lucky individuals who were selected as the first tourists to visit the island."

The cameraman zoomed past the young reporter and homed in on a small crowd of people congregated behind a small wooden fence. An Indian man and his wife stared intently at the camera as if the operator had intruded on a private event. Beside them stood a middle-aged woman in an ill-fitting bikini who had scrawled the message "Basingstoke conquers the world" across her bare midriff. Next to her stood a gaunt-looking man in his 30s. He was holding up a piece of cardboard on which he had written a message. At first, the cameraman was positioned at an angle where the sign was illegible but as the cameraman zoomed in ever closer, Claudia was able to see that the message was addressed to her. "Claudia! Read my email!" Her heart skipped a beat as she realized that the scruffy looking male holding the tacky looking placard was none other than a recently fired journalist Padraig Coyle. "So you are my dark cloud," said Claudia quietly as she thought back to the horoscope. With another click of her mouse, she minimized the still babbling reporter and opened up her email inbox.

All of the messages in her inbox had been read except for two. Both of those emails were from the same author. Feeling frustrated, Claudia clicked on the trash can icon and deleted the first of Padraig's e-mails. She moved her cursor a few millimeters further down the screen and clicked on the trash can icon for a second time. I have no interest in his insane ramblings, she thought to herself as she attempted to dispatch his article into the cyber world abyss. However, things didn't go to plan. The second email was still on the screen. She clicked on it again and again but still, it remained in her inbox like a defiant child refusing to leave the room. Once more she attempted to erase the offending e-mail and finally, her pc responded but not in the manner she had been hoping for. "Program not responding," said the textbox that appeared in the center of the screen.

Either her PC or the network as a whole had decided to spare Padraig's e-mail by choosing this very moment to crash. Claudia had a reputation for being a no-nonsense boss. Despite her reputation for pragmatism, she had inherited a superstitious streak from her Sicilian ancestors. She couldn't remember the last time the office PC had crashed. Whether she liked it or not, somebody or something didn't want to delete that email. She had no real idea what it contained. She had absolute contempt for the man who wrote it but in her mind, she now felt that she would have to read it. First of all though, she would have to wait for her PC to reset itself. While that was going on she may as well go to lunch. If fate intended for her to do something, she always felt obliged to do it. Although, she didn't see anything wrong with making fate or any other kind of mysterious force wait for a while before she reluctantly complied with its wishes.

Aqua Monde was ready for its official launch. All of the paying guests and the visiting dignitaries had been ushered into the large conference hall that was located at the far end of the swimming area. The hall could hold a thousand people. Less than half that number were inside today as room had been cleared for a large octagonal platform to be installed in the center of the room.

On the platform sat a glass dome about the size of a small removal truck. A dim blue light lit the globe from the interior. Strategically placed laser lights around the hall were projecting images of the world's continents onto the glass ball. Video images were projected onto each country to give the viewers an idea of life around the Earth. Footage of kangaroos hopping around could be seen in the Australian section of the globe while Inuits built a temporary shelter from ice blocks in the Canadian section. A recording of the first suite of Handel's water music bellowed out from speakers that hung menacingly from the ceiling.

The first few rows of seats were occupied by the advanced party who had been on the island for a few days. The Patels, the Bradshaws and most of the rest of the group sat sullen faced as the music and light show continued. Behind them, the newcomers to the island were rather more enthusiastic. Every flicker of light or musical crescendo was greeted with gasps and applause. As the section of music finally reached an end, the lights dimmed.

The hall was in darkness. Suddenly, a brilliant beam of white light burst down from the roof and caused the glass globe to sparkle like a snowflake caught between the Earth and the sun. A husky-voiced man began to speak over the tannoy. Billy was sure it was Morgan Freeman's voice. "They said it couldn't be done," he said as the white light dimmed and images of the ocean began to appear all over the globe. "A team of the world's greatest scientists and engineers were determined to prove the cynics wrong. They had a common dream. A dream of a world in which children in the poorest of nations could have daily access to clean water. They had a dream of a world in which man could reclaim land from the sea and live without fear of the rising oceans. They had a dream that involved building the largest structure in human history in order to revive the memory of a continent that was lost to history eons ago. These men had a dream and their dream is now your reality."

As the narrator finished his dramatic introduction, images of the resort appeared on the globe alongside footage of whales bursting out of the ocean and African children pumping water from a well. Most of the audience rose to their feet as they applauded the audiovisual display. The Patels were unmoved.

At the far end of the hall, Jim Boyle stood in a doorway watching the whole scene unfold. Sweat was running uncontrollably from his scalp, down his forehead, and into his eyes. He rubbed his fists into his eyes but as he did so the sense of moistness was replaced with stinging pain. "You'll mess up your makeup," said Cathy Furman who was busy attaching his microphone to his lapel. "I don't see why the makeup is necessary," moaned Boyle. "Because if you go out there without it you'll look like a ghost." A young man holding a clipboard appeared from the corridor behind them and gestured at Boyle. "You're on pal!" he said. Before he had a chance to react, Boyle found himself caught in the glare of a spotlight that seemed to be drawing him towards the stage. Reluctantly, he began to make his way towards the podium that was located directly in front of the glass globe.

The crowd's cheering seemed to calm his nerves. He started to pump his fist in the air as he neared the stage. He allowed the excited onlookers to give him a lengthy ovation before he eventually began to speak. "Ladies and gentlemen. Welcome to Aqua Monde." Another round of excited applause spread through the room. "This was a huge undertaking for Aqua monde and our corporate sponsors. Our dynamic team of professionals used cutting-edge technology to ensure that the whole process was seamless." Boyle paused to allow the exuberant audience to show their appreciation once again.

The viewers in the first row were less than impressed. "He's having a laugh ain't it?" asked Billy of Sam who simply shrugged by way of response. Aside from the disgruntled guests in the first few rows, another group of onlookers were less than impressed with Boyle's attempts to deceive the more recent arrivals about the state of play on the island.

Padraig, Danny, and Hewlett couldn't see the speaker but they could hear his voice. The trio were lying head to toe in the ventilation shaft that was embedded in the lower section of the wall at the back of the auditorium. Beneath the narrow gaps in the metal sheeting, Padraig could see the backs of some of the people who were seemingly in awe of Boyle. He couldn't see much else. He daren't speak for fear of arousing suspicion although a whisper in a vent would have been hard to hear above the din being created in the hall.

"We are honored to have many visiting dignitaries here with us today," Boyle continued "and I'd like to extend our warm wishes to all of you but at this time, I'd like to hand the podium over to a distinguished guest. Prince Faisal bin Ahmed was one of the visionaries who saw the potential in the first blueprints for this structure. When others shied away from commitment, the prince boldly invested in this project and his dream, like ours, has finally been realized. Ladies and gentlemen may I present Prince Faisal bin Ahmed."

Everyone, including the cynics in the first few rows, felt compelled to stand and applaud for the royal visitor. The blindingly bright spotlight shifted to the far end of the room. The doorway used for the Prince's entrance was just a few inches from the vent where Padraig was hidden. Boyle let out a deep sigh as the stage dimmed. He had managed to keep his composure. He was feeling quite pleased with himself considering the kind of week he had endured. All he had to do now was make sure Faisal made it safely to the platform, then he could smile for a few pictures before disappearing to his office and having a well-earned smoke.

Faisal was in no hurry. The diminutive prince was eager to enjoy his moment in the limelight. He was eagerly shaking hands with male members of the audience as he slowly meandered his way down the hall. Faisal, like the four guards that accompanied him was dressed in traditional robes and a headdress. Despite being inside he was wearing sunglasses although they were proving quite useful in terms of protecting his eyes against the unforgiving glare of the spotlight. Faisal had, in fact, had very little involvement in the construction of the island. He was a playboy. He liked to gamble. Aqua Monde just happened to be one of his few gambles that actually paid off. He had actually invested twice as much in another scheme to start commercial space flights. The company behind that plan had folded just months before construction had been completed on Aqua Monde. Nevertheless, as a major shareholder, the prince was only too happy to accept the adulation from the excited crowd.

After what to Boyle had seemed like hours, Faisal finally completed his trek to the stage. He marked his arrival by giving the American a long and lingering handshake that seemed to last almost as long as his slow stroll to the podium. Boyle wondered if the prince had suffered a mild stroke and whether an involuntary muscle spasm was to blame for the seemingly unending handclasp. Finally, the prince released the American's hand and stepped up to the microphone.

"Thank you," he said. Those two words lead to another 60 seconds of wild applause. The audience were in a rock concert style frenzy. This small modestly dressed man was the star of the show. Boyle had decided to stay on the podium alongside the prince while he gave his speech but after surviving his own spell in the spotlight he was ready to vacate the premises.

As Faisal began to exaggerate his own involvement in the project, Boyle quietly stepped off the stage. He hastily made his way to the nearest exit. As he burst through the fire escape doors, he collided with a tall, frail-looking man with fair hair. "I'm sorry," he said before rushing off without giving the man a second glance. The man in question failed to react either to the collision or to Boyle's begrudging apology. He was in a trance-like state. His eyes transfixed on the man on the stage.

"As a boy, I always wanted to build something that I could be proud of." Faisal was ad-libbing a creation story for Aqua Monde that had him involved at every stage of development. The previously enthusiastic audience were now tiring. The exuberant cheers were now being replaced with occasional bursts of polite applause. As the audience became more muted, the prince tried even harder to stir their emotions with fantastical tales of his own engineering genius. All the while, the man who had passed Boyle in the doorway slowly and deliberately made his way towards the stage.

The audience began to murmur as the mysterious man made his way down the aisle. Their muttering became so loud that it caught the attention of the Aqua Monde employees who were watching the speech from the rear of the auditorium.
"Who the hell is that" whispered Cathy Furman to Kevin Newman who until that point had been tinkering with his cellphone. Even with glasses, Newman's vision was poor. He winced as he tried to focus on the figure who was at least 40 yards away and barely visible in the darkened room.
"I have no idea."
"That's not the point!" snapped Furman "I don't care WHO he is. I just want to know WHY he is strolling down the hallway towards

our esteemed guest speaker."
"Oh," replied Newman meekly. "Erm, I am not sure. Maybe we should send some security guys down there to stop him." Furman rolled her eyes as Newman fumbled around in his jacket pocket trying to find his walkie-talkie. As he did so, the man in question suddenly became illuminated as he walked between Faisal and one of the many spotlights that had been pointed in his direction. As the light shone upon him the tall figure turned and cast a steely gaze over the watching audience.
"No," said Newman "It can't be!" Even Newman with his poor eyesight was able to recognize a well-lit face from that distance. "It's Henrik!" he exclaimed "but he was …"
"Dead," replied Furman.

Like those all around him, Faisal was puzzled to see the lanky Norwegian strolling towards the stage. He stopped his speech mid-sentence and turned away from the lectern to greet Henrik who was now just a few feet away.
Covering the microphone with his hand the prince spoke sternly to the uninvited guest.
"Please, will you go and take your seat!" Henrik stopped walking and just stared at the prince for a moment as if he was pondering his next move.
"Take him back to his seat," said Faisal to his bewildered guards.

As the quartet edged towards the Norwegian Henrik violently flung his head backward before throwing it forward with equal force and unleashing a mouthful of phlegm in the direction of the royal speaker. Faisal was stunned. He lost his balance and stumbled to his knees as he instinctively pulled his hands to his face and attempted to wipe away the icy feeling liquid.

The sticky phlegm had covered his nose and his mouth. As his fingers made contact with the spittal it immediately hardened into a plasticky film that covered the central section of his face. With his mouth and his nostrils entirely covered the prince suddenly became aware that he couldn't breathe. He began desperately clawing at the phlegm blocking his air ducts as his guards closed in on Henrik.

Everyone's attention had shifted from the prince to the Norwegian. Nobody noticed as the prince slumped back onto the floor. The nearest guard to Henrik placed a firm hand on his shoulder. As he did so he felt a sensation like a pinprick piercing the tip of his forefinger. Despite the slight discomfort that it caused he kept his hand in place and instructed Henrik to turn and leave the room.

The other three guards pulled pistols from their holsters and indicated that Henrik should comply with their comrade's instructions. Henrik had other ideas. The guard who had gripped his shoulder was the first to suffer. An icy numb sensation raced through his fingers, up his arms, and into his chest. An immense pressure built up in the man's rib cage. It felt as if his heart had been placed in a vice. He let out a shrill scream before releasing his grip on the Scandinavian and falling flat on his back. He was dead.

The other three guards, alarmed at his collapse and unsure of the reason began unloading their weapons in the direction of Henrik. Pandemonium erupted all around them as the guests fled for the exits. Edith who had been sitting with her group in the front row pointed towards the door through which Boyle had exited and quickly led her group to safety. Other guests fought and pushed their way towards the doors at the back of the hall.
There was absolute mayhem as manners were forgotten. The strongest men in the room brushed past the frail and the elderly to make their way toward safety.

Despite a few dozen bullets having been fired in his direction Henrik was unmoved. The last of the guards exhausted his supply of bullets by firing three shots at Henrik's chest from point-blank range. A small puff of smoke oozed from the center of the Norwegian's chest as the bullets made contact with his body. He neither flinched nor reacted in any way as the guards stood wondering what kind of unearthly fiend they were confronting.

Driven by a mixture of curiosity and wonder, the guard who had just finished pummeling bullets into Henrik leant forward. He poked his forefinger into the black and crispy wound that had opened up in the center of Henrik's chest. He pushed his finger further and further until there was no fleshy resistance at all and the tip of his finger emerged through the center of Henrik's back. Shocked and horrified he withdrew his finger and turned to his colleagues who had watched his investigative prodding in stunned silence. Nothing was said but the trio knew that it was time to run. However, after a few minutes of absolute stillness, Henrik was on the move again. He raised both arms and stretched his fingers out in front of him as if he were preparing to dive into a pool. The guards weren't interested in waiting to see what he had in mind. The three of them stumbled over the lifeless body of their paymaster and made their way towards the exit.

Edith's group were still making their way through as the three Arabian guards came charging over. The armed men were frantically waving their hands in the air and muttering all kinds of obscenities as they desperately tried to shove their way to freedom. Like a hawk waiting to seize his prey, Henrik stood watching the mob by the door. His outstretched hands shuddered slightly as he unleashed ten small projectiles from beneath the skin of his skeletal fingertips.

The commotion at the door suddenly calmed down as the 10 unlucky souls who had yet to make their way through the exit and stopped in their tracks as bullets of ice pierced the back of their skulls. Edith who had already made it through the doorway didn't see what had happened. She realized it was time to slam the door shut as 10 pairs of eyes rolled back into the heads of the people she'd been holding the door for. Faisal's guards and a handful of her own tour group crumpled to the floor in a heap as she slammed the door shut.

Edith turned to the fortunate folk who had made it out alive. Stunned and confused, the Patels, Bradshaws and the rest of her group stared expectantly in her direction. "Ladies and gentlemen," in a remarkably calm voice "I am not sure what is going on but I suggest that we leave this area as quickly as we can." For once no one in her group was going to argue.

In the hall, Henrik was making his way towards the groups of people crowding around the two exits at the back of the room. He slowly walked down the center aisle with one hand pointed towards each door. all the while firing ice pellets from the tips of his fingers. The panicked guests pushed and shoved as they scrambled for the exits. The jostling became more frantic as Henrik's victims became obstacles that blocked the way of the living. Piles of bodies accumulated by each set of doors. The last of the survivors had to climb over corpses as they scurried their way through the exit.

The hall was finally plunged into silence as the last living humans made their way through the exits and slammed the hall doors shut. While the crowds had gone, their fumbled screams could still be heard as panicked souls collided with one another in the hallways.

In a vent at the back of the hall, Padraig, Danny, and Beauchamp had heard the commotion but had been unable to see the drama unfold. They had no idea that Henrik was still inside the hall. They had no way of knowing that he had single-handedly struck down dozens of guests, reporters, and visiting dignitaries. "What happened?" whispered Danny. He hoped that at least one of the other men had been able to see more than he had through the gaps in the vent. Neither Beauchamp nor Padraig had been able to see anything other than running feet and chairs being knocked to the floor.
"I don't know," said Padraig "but it was something bad. Something very, very bad," he continued, " I think we ought to get out of here."

The ventilation shaft had not been designed to accommodate people. The trio were laying flat on their faces, head-to-toe in the shaft. There wasn't sufficient room for them to turn around and head back to the open vent through which they had crawled. Danny who had been the last to enter the shaft would be the first to exit. He awkwardly began to shuffle feet first towards the exit. He was somewhat wary of what may lay on the other side of the entrance. He didn't much like the thought that his head would be the last part of his body to emerge into the open. As much as was possible, he balled himself up before quickly thrusting himself through the opening. He jumped to his feet and scanned the hallway. Thankfully, he was alone. Beauchamp was the next to emerge and as he stretched his weary limbs, Padraig gingerly emerged from the shaft. He'd caught his right knee on a stray nail whilst crawling in the dark. Although there were plenty of other dangers on the island he found himself struggling to remember the last time he'd had a tetanus shot. Had it been five years, 10? Maybe even longer. Seeing that the journalist was engrossed in his own thoughts, Danny snapped his fingers to bring his attention back to their immediate predicament.

"What now?" asked Danny.
"I'd rather like to take a look in the hall to see exactly what happened in there," said Beauchamp. Padraig and Danny weren't so sure that Beauchamp's plan represented a good idea.
"Whatever happened in there led to a lot of gunshots, screaming, and commotion," reasoned Padraig, "everyone who was in there ran away in terror. I am not sure that it is such a good idea to go bursting in there."
"It sounded to me as if everyone was running away from something so it is safe to assume that whatever or whoever was chasing them probably left the hall when they did." Beauchamp's counter argument seemed fairly logical. Padraig looked at Danny whose noncommittal shrug was as good as a nod to the Beauchamp.

The veteran security man seized the initiative. He made his way down the hallway towards the doors that hordes of terrified people had rushed through just moments before. As the trio neared the entrance, the doors suddenly swung open. Unsure of what would emerge. All three men pushed themselves flat against the wall. Danny clenched his fist. Padraig held his breath. Beauchamp mentally prepared himself to see the unexpected. Despite his best efforts, the old man found himself gasping in disbelief as Henrik made his way out into the hallway. The last time Beauchamp had seen him, Henrik had been loaded into a body bag. Yet here he was, calmly strolling into the hallway.

Danny and Padraig, unaware of Henrik's earlier demise, relaxed and stepped away from the wall once it became apparent that the Norwegian was unarmed. Henrik, they assumed, must have hidden from whatever it was that had been in the hall.
"What happened in there?" asked Padraig as he made his way towards Henrik "we heard all of the commotion." The journalist's march towards the newest arrival in the corridor was abruptly halted. Beauchamp forcefully blocked his progress by flinging out an arm in

front of him. Henrik, who had been looking towards the journalist turned toward the Security Chief. "I don't know who … or what he is," said Beauchamp quietly "but gentlemen," he said turning to Padraig and Danny "this man was dead. I saw him lifeless and covered in blood."

Danny scoffed "He looks pretty alive to me."
Padraig was more diplomatic, "maybe you were mistaken."
"No," said Beauchamp "I know this man. His name is Henrik. He was part of the archaeological dig team and I saw him stuffed into a body bag just yesterday."
Beauchamp's gaze was now entirely focused on Henrik although his rigid arm was serving as an effective barrier to stop Padraig getting any nearer to the one-time archaeologist.

Padraig turned and looked towards Danny who was a few feet further down the hallway. Danny raised his right forefinger to his head and made a circling motion to indicate that Beauchamp may have lost his sense of reason. Over the past few days, Padraig had developed a pretty good rapport with the recently fired Security Chief. He had no reason to think that Beauchamp was either a fantasist or a lunatic. With that being said, he had covered stories before in which previously rational people had been driven to insanity as a result of stress or trauma. Perhaps the strain of the job loss, the torture of Flomo and the ruckus in the hall had driven Beauchamp mad.

"Maybe you're right," said Padraig sympathetically "but maybe you'd feel better if you had a sit-down." Beauchamp slammed his fist against the wall before turning and glaring at the journalist "I may have lost my job but I have not lost my marbles!" As the last syllable rolled off his tongue Henrik who to this point had been motionless suddenly raised his right hand in the air. Beauchamp realized something was going on behind him as he saw Padraig and Danny look up into the air. The old man spun around only for Henrik to plunge a glistening shard of ice into his throat. Startled, Padraig backed away and quickly found himself cowering behind Danny. Beauchamp slunk towards the ground as blood splattered from his pierced veins onto Henrik's shirt and the hallway walls.

Danny looked around for something that he could use as a weapon but the corridor was empty. His fists would have to do, he rushed towards the Norwegian. As he swung his arm back and prepared to unleash a punch he noticed that Henrik's chest was peppered with holes. How could he be walking around when he looked as if several rounds of bullets had passed through his chest? If bullets couldn't harm this guy then fisticuffs were also likely to be ineffective. Danny had already decided to abandon his plan of attack when Padraig too noticed the bullet holes. Grabbing Danny's jacket he pulled his friend away from the abnormal Norwegian. "Let's get the hell out of here."

Henrik swung his right arm in Danny's direction but the force with which Padraig jerked him meant that he fell back at an opportune moment. Henrik's jagged ice blade struck the wall rather than his head. Thankful to have avoided contact, Danny steadied himself and then sprinted after Padraig down the hallway. Unphased, Henrik retrieved his blade from the wall and after inspecting his weapon he stepped over the bloodied corpse of Beauchamp and slowly began to make his way down the hallway.

Padraig burst through the swing doors at the far end of the hallway and found himself in the main reception area of the resort. Danny, struggling to catch his breath stumbled into him as he came flying through the same doorway. Padraig looked back through the small oval window on the door. Henrik was at least 50-yards behind them and was walking slowly and deliberately in their direction.

The reception area was full of doors leading to different parts of the resort. It was time to pick a route before Beauchamp's slayer caught up with them. On the far side of the room was a glass escalator that moved in a downwards direction to bring people from the second floor into the lobby area. "That way," said Padraig pointing at the moving staircase. "With the speed that he walks at he'd never be able to get up a downwards escalator."

Gasping for breath, Danny wasn't convinced that he would be able to defy gravity and scale the escalator himself. Before he had time to vocalize his thoughts Padraig had already sprinted across the floor and was swiftly making his way up the moving glass steps. Danny inhaled deeply before following his friend up the escalator. The duo reached the top before their pursuer made it into the lobby. Without hesitation, they ran through the nearest set of swing doors and found themselves in another long corridor.

Numbered doors lined both sides of the hallway. This area was a bit more grim looking than the guest area where the duo had been assigned a room. "Staff rooms?" suggested Danny. Padraig didn't respond and instead started scurrying towards the fire door at the end of the narrow hallway. A sign on the door read "keep closed except in emergencies."
"I hope it is not alarmed," said Padraig "don't want our friend to find where we are!"

Before Danny had a chance to second guess his plan the journalist turned the handle and opened the door. Silence. No alarm. "Phew," said Padraig. As he walked through the door the sensation of something tugging at his shirt startled him. He spun around to see a familiar face standing on the other side of the doorway.

"Hello stranger," said Anne. Mindful of the threat posed by Henrik, Danny forced the duo out of his way and shoved his way through the door. They were now at the top of a downward moving escalator that was presumably designed as an escape route to be used during emergencies. Glancing down towards ground level, Danny thought that this might be one emergency in which it was best to stay upstairs.

Having surveyed the scene he turned towards Anne and noticed that Flomo was standing behind her. "I thought you had left the resort," he said.
"We did," replied Flomo "but we nicked the boat they were going to send us home on. Idiots left the keys on board. We made our way back to the far side of the resort so we could finish what we had set out to do."
"Which is what?" asked Padraig.
"Find out what the hell is going on here," snapped Anne. "We just

saw a whole mob of people running through here screaming and crying."

"Some people were killed," said Padraig.

"I know," replied Anne "some of my friends were among them. Some of my dig team, Henrik, and the guys from the boat were among them."

"Henrik?" asked Padraig.

"Yes," said Anne. "You guys didn't meet him but he was one of my team. A really sweet Norwegian guy."

"Erm I am not quite sure how to put this," Padraig said awkwardly "but he's not dead anymore."

"You trying to be funny?" snapped Anne. "That idiot Beauchamp had him arrested for some reason and he died while in custody."

"Well as of now," replied Padraig, "he is alive again and in fact, he just killed said Security Chief."

Anne was aghast. Clearly, Padraig's tale was difficult to believe but time was of the essence so he had to get the message across to Anne as quickly as he could. Padraig looked hopefully at Flomo for support but the African reacted with annoyance.

"Why are you looking at me?"

"Well you … well I mean you can …" Padraig couldn't verbalize his thought process.

"I can reassure her that you're right and that her friend has become a zombie?" Flomo finished Padraig's sentence for him.

"Well, yeah," said Padraig awkwardly.

"I am Liberian mate, not Haitian. I don't believe in zombies or things that go bump in the night any more than she does."

Before Padraig could respond the sound of footsteps echoing from ground level caught their attention. Everyone peered over the balcony and it quickly became apparent that no further explanations would be necessary. Nonetheless, Danny felt the need to state the obvious. "Well," he said "as you can see for yourself. Henrik is back on his feet." To Anne's horror, the young Norwegian was slowly making his way towards the exit door less than 30-feet below the landing on which they were standing.

Lunch was over and after enjoying a green salad, two large coffees and a glass of mineral water, Claudia was ready to get back to work. She shuffled her mouse around to bring her PC back to life. After typing in her password she was ready to peruse Padraig's email. She lined up her cursor over the message from the errant reporter and was about to hit "open" when her phone started to ring. Glancing at the caller display she noticed that the caller was her boss, Jeff Sanchez. Padraig's email would have to wait.
"Jeff," she said after tapping the speakerphone button at the base of the phone.
"Claudia, don't you have an entertainment reporter in Aqua Monde," asked the deep voice on the other end of the phone.
"Yes," she replied apprehensively as she wondered why her boss had taken a sudden interest in the man-made island.
"Well have you heard from him yet?" demanded Sanchez.
"About what exactly?"
"About the incident," said Sanchez who was becoming increasingly exasperated.

Claudia had no idea what he was talking about but she had obviously missed something while she was at lunch. Rather than ask her temperamental boss for clarification she quickly directed her PC's browser to her firm's 24-hour news chAnnel. The major headline caused her jaw to drop. "Terrorist attack at Aqua Monde. Many dead." Her thoughts immediately turned to Padraig and his efforts to inform her of a "scoop" that he'd been working on. Was the incident somehow connected to the shenanigans that he had uncovered? Without further delay she opened his email and began scanning the content to see what the English hack had been so desperate to share with her.

In the first few lines of text the words "terrorist" "arrest" and "injustice" caught her attention. "Well, are you there?" Sanchez's voice bellowed out of the phone set.
"Yes," she replied "let me call you back. I am just getting some info now from my man on the scene." She hung up the phone before Sanchez had a chance to ask any more questions. Having scanned the email for keywords, she started to read it again from the beginning only this time she actually made an effort to digest the content as a whole.

The story as Padraig told it concerned an activist from Liberia being wrongly portrayed as a "terrorist" by a global firm that had misled the U.N. and pushed poor people over the edge into abject poverty. There wasn't any suggestion in Padraig's report that this "Flomo" guy or his cohorts were in any way dangerous or violent. However, Padraig wouldn't be the first reporter to get duped into characterizing violent extremists as political activists.

She minimized the email and turned up the volume on the video stream on the 24-hour newsfeed. The U.S. based anchor was talking about Aqua Monde but the only footage they were showing was stock video from the publicity material. Presumably, there were no cameras running when the drama unfolded. Either that or someone had decided that the images were too graphic to show on TV.

"If you're just tuning in now," said the male anchor in a somber voice "we are awaiting further details at this hour but there are reports that terrorists have conducted an operation on the man-made island Aqua Monde. Prince Faisal of the Emirates who was one of the major financiers behind the project is believed to be among the dead. As we understand it, up to a dozen people may have been killed by the assassin or assassins. These reports are based upon information that was received via telephone from family members of employees who work on the island. At this time, communications with the resort have been disrupted and it is unclear whether that is due to atmospheric conditions or some other cause. We will bring you more details as we receive that information."

Claudia had read enough to piece together a version of events that made sense to her. She had her Sanchez's number on speed dial and within the space of a few seconds, she had her boss back on the line.
"Well?" he said by way of a greeting.
"OK. The terrorists were Liberians who were trying to draw attention to the fact that AM corp was siphoning water out of North West Africa while passing themselves off as the great white hope that was actually supposedly providing fresh drinking water to the continent. My man actually encountered one of these people. The security team at the resort obviously had a pretty good idea that something like this might happen because they arrested several people who were deemed to be dangerous just last night."

She finished her summary and she was expecting a few words of praise from her boss. His reaction was not quite what she had expected. "I see," he said calmly. "Look, Claudia, this is what you're going to do. You're going to keep this business about the water issue to yourself because it is not in our best interests to go there. The West Africans, - you know and I know that there are Islamic groups in that part of the world."
"These folks are from Liberia," interrupted Claudia "they are Christians, animists, atheists. Some Muslims but they are not typically radicals in that neck of the woods. Anyway, this is all about money and water, not religion."
"I didn't say it was about religion," replied Sanchez "but it wouldn't do any harm if you presented it in such a way that people thought … it might be. People want to know why things happen and we're not touching the water so go with the religious angle otherwise we're

going to get into trouble."

"I don't understand," said Claudia "we have the facts behind the story so why wouldn't I just publish the scoop that we have, warts and all?"

"Look," replied Sanchez coldly "you're a smart, attractive woman. You've a nice family, a good job and decent career prospects. Let's not do anything to change any of that."

Claudia felt cold as if someone had just sucked all of the blood out of her body. "Are you threatening me?" she asked nervously. Despite everything she had just heard she somehow hoped against hope that this was all a big misunderstanding and that her boss was going to set things straight.

"I'm being straight with you," he replied, "write it with the angle that I said and you'll be able to sleep safe and sound in your own bed tonight."

The phone line buzzed as Sanchez hung up the receiver. What did Sanchez know that she didn't know? Assuming Padraig was still alive, what might he have learnt since he sent his last email? The picture of her daughters that she kept on her desk told her that she had no choice but to comply with Sanchez's instructions. While she couldn't yet print the truth, nothing was put in place to prevent her trying to learn more about the truth. Somehow, she had to try and get in touch with Padraig.

EXODUS

Following her own instincts, Edith had led her tour group out of the resort complex and into the as yet undeveloped area that included the archaeological site. The cave that Anne's team had been excavating would have made a good hiding place but aside from the fact that it had been flooded, the entrance to the dig site had been sealed with a heavy-weight padlock. Rather than heading back towards the mayhem in the resort, Edith opted to go around the fenced in area. She finally allowed her group to catch their breath in a muddy area directly behind the dig site.

Small black rocks poked out of the soft ground. Several of the weary travelers decided to use the rocks as makeshift stools. Unlike the rest of the group, the drama of the day had given Billy Bradshaw a shot of adrenalin. He decided to expend some of his energy by exploring the area. The land was largely featureless aside from a few clusters of rocks. In the distance, a large wall prevented the ocean from reclaiming the patch of land that had previously been under water.

Despite the lack of obvious points of interest, Bradshaw wandered away from the group and started making his way towards the perimeter wall. A passing flock of seagulls caught his attention and he instinctively ducked as if fearing a repeat of the exploding seagull incident that had traumatized the travelers while they were at sea. The birds flew towards him and flapped their wings just inches over his head as if they were taunting him. Bradshaw responded in kind by flapping his own appendages around in the air above his head until the birds eventually tired of the taunting and began to move off. Satisfied that the danger had passed, Bradshaw straightened up. As he did so his left foot slipped on the moist ground beneath him and he found himself sliding into the splits position. Bradshaw dropped the Aqua Monde brochure he had been planning to use as a makeshift truncheon and dropped his hands to the ground before completing his descent into the splits position. Letting out a small sigh of relief, he steadied himself and got back on his feet.

While he was not typically someone who was concerned about littering, the starkness of the area drew attention to the brochure he had dropped. Not wanting to draw more attention to himself than he already had he decided he ought to pick it up again. Aside from anything else, when folded up it could deliver quite a firm whack to anyone who threatened his person. He reached down to get it but before he had a chance to grip it, a blast of boiling liquid shot up from the ground beneath it. Gravity caused the brownish sludge to return to the Earth and a thick dollop of wet mud landed on his brochure. The slight weight of the substance caused the glossy corporate publication to sink beneath the surface of the Earth.

Unnerved, Bradshaw looked at the ground below him and to his relief he saw that he was standing on a jagged patch of rock. The area immediately beside him though was a steaming mud bath. "Quicksand" said the Englishman as if he had made a unique discovery. "Volcanic discharges," said a voice from over his shoulder. It was Mike Patel who after a moment of relaxation had found himself as full of nervous energy as Bradshaw. "I wouldn't get too close," said the Indian "this stuff could melt the skin off your body."
"I was going to dive right in," said Bradshaw defiantly"what do you take me for? A right idiot?" Patel politely smiled before turning and walking back towards his still resting cohorts.

The sound of boots pounding over volcanic rock startled the group. Everyone was on edge after the bloodbath during the opening ceremony. To their relief, the footsteps signaled the arrival of a trio of security guards and a familiar face. "Well Hell Mr. Patel," yelled Owen Gaunt "I know you're wary about investing but surely the last few days have convinced you of the need to buy some good life insurance coverage!"

As ever, Gaunt's quip was received a mixture of grimaces and disconcerting looks. Mike Patel attempted to apply some logic to the situation as he feigned interest in Gaunt's proposal. "You're right Mr. Gaunt. Life is precarious, especially during this so-called vacation. But before you sign me up, please ensure the contract doesn't have exclusions for death by zombie."
Gaunt found himself unusually short for words. He had expected his mock bravado and gallows humor to be met with disgust. He hadn't expected anyone to make an equally dark quip in response. Edith, unaware of their simmering rivalry, was focussed on the safety of the

group. "What is the situation back there Mr. Gaunt?" she asked, "I trust the security guys have the situation under control."

Gaunt smiled. She had given him the perfect cue to get back to his typically hyperbolic, offensive schtick. "Not at all," Gaunt chuckled, "it is a bloodbath in there. It is like turkey farm at Thanksgiving. Only this butcher has more holes in him than the Last Jedi screenplay." Billy was alarmed.
"I saw those guys get off a few shots at point blank range. That nutter's got to be dead."
"I counted 400 rounds," replied Gaunt having multiplied reality by the power of 10. "The bullets went right through him like water through a sieve."
"That is ridiculous," scoffed Patel, "obviously he had some kind of body armor. This must be some kind of terrorist attack."
"Nope" said Gaunt dismissively "the only 'terrorist' we had here was a Liberian fellow who loaded up the water pipes with cattle's blood. The kid doing the killing was a Norwegian kid. Probably one of these death metal socialist nuts."
"So what are we to do?" asked Sam in exasperation.
"It's simple," replied Gaunt, "the way I see it. This guy can take a bullet so there is no point shooting him. But I've never seen any kind of body armour that can withstand molten lava at 2,000 degrees Fahrenheit. We get someone to lure the son of a bitch out here and shove him into one of these boiling potholes."

Edith was unimpressed "and I take it you won't be volunteering for the task of playing Bugs Bunny to Elmer Thud?"
"No ma'am," Gaunt responded. "I have a back injury I picked up during the Gulf War. It inhibits my velocity when running."
"You fought in the Gulf War?" asked Mike Patel incredulously.
"I didn't say I fought," mumbled Gaunt. "I picked it up at the time of the Gulf war. Clearing heavy boxes from my garage."

Billy had heard enough."Look smart ass I think we've all heard enough of your nonsense. This bloke is armed and dangerous. None of us is stupid enough to go running in there and ask him to run out here so you can try and shove him down the volcano."
Patel concurred with Bradshaw but his memory of the event deviated

in one crucial detail. "I don't remember seeing the man holding a weapon per se. It looked like he was throwing some kind of glass projectiles," suggested Patel "maybe glass Ninja flying stars."

"Well." Gaunt interrupted "that is where this smart ass can correct you. Those weren't glass, they were ice. Good old H20. The same thing that killed old Pompidou. Sharp and dense enough to pierce skin and organs but quickly melted by body warmth after impact."

"Again with the nonsense," yelled Edith.

For once, Gaunt was telling the truth. "It is true," chimed in the nearest security guard. "We retrieved the bodies from the auditorium. There was no glass or any other other substance. Just the entry wound and the clothing around the wounds was drenched in ice cold water."

"Oh lovely," exclaimed Billy "I'll tell you something, I've been on some dodgy holidays in my time but this takes the biscuit. Bloody wasp nests at Butlins in Torbay, Delhi Belly in Skegness, cabaret act banging my misses in Bognor but in all my years I have never had to put up with the Ice Man knocking off my traveling companions. So I don't want to speak for the rest of you, but this holiday is a bloody disaster. And before Spiderman and the Incredible Hulk show up for a battle over the volcano with Ice Man, I say we only have one course of action: find a bloody big boat and get the hell out of here."

The security guards smirked at Billy's suggestion but in doing so they provoked the ire of Mike Patel. "He is absolutely right," said Patel. "This is an island. Presumably, the primary form of transport here is a boat. That is assuming none of us want to risk another Seagull attack and hijack a helicopter."

Regardless of her pitiful wage, Edith was becoming alarmed at the mob mentality surfacing in the group. Despite everything, she feared that on some level she would get a dressing down, when and if things returned to normal. "Please, please ladies and gentleman," she begged "let us calm ourselves down. We are in the middle of the Atlantic. We can't just requisition a ship or a yacht and set off for the high seas."

"A yacht!" cried Patel as if he was having a Eureka moment. "Well of course. You're absolutely right. I was thinking in terms of the ship that brought us here but a yacht would be much easier and more maneuverable. What a great suggestion!"

Edith's attempt at calming the group had spectacularly backfired. Instantaneously, everyone present began rattling off the names of celebrity visitors who 'probably' arrived by yacht. Though no one in the group had prior experience of manning such a craft, the consensus was that it would be easier to steer than a cruise liner. "How hard can it be?" proffered Owen Gaunt. As the group coalesced around the boat hijack plan, Edith looked to the security guards for support. Regretfully, they had no more desire to stay on the island than anyone else. It was decided, the rag-tag group would steal a yacht and sail to freedom.

Everyone converged around Mike Patel who had assumed an unofficial leadership role. It was time to find a boat. The sound of automatic doors opening caught everyone's attention. A new face had arrived upon the scene. Slowly making his way towards the group was a man everyone immediately recognized. It was Prince Faisal.

The special events banquet hall was a hive of activity. Security staff had ushered panicked guests from the hall into the vast, elegantly decorated venue. Chandeliers glistened overhead while bloodied and terrified resort guests cowered beneath. It was like a scene from the London Underground during the blitz. Unlikely pairings of people thrown together by a calamitous event. Pop stars and famous athletes used napkins and mineral water to clean the wounds of hotel staff and security guards.

In the center of the makeshift camp stood Cathy Furman. Along with Kevin Newman she was hastily distributing bottled water to the traumatized survivors. Ever the professional, her beaming smile disguised her own sense of terror. At the far end of the room, Boyle exchanged some notes with the security guards before heading over to his colleagues.

"This room is totally secure," Boyle informed Furman, "We

overrode the magnetic access panels. Nobody can get in and nobody can get out. We will be safe here."

The bulletproof windows and steel reinforced walls ensured nobody could break in through unconventional means.

"Your archaeologist friends really are Hell-bent on putting us out of business aren't they Kevin?" Boyle sneered.

"Jim," pleaded Kevin "Henrik was dead. He was in a body bag. The Doctor said every drop of blood had been drained from his body."

"And yet he was able to barge into the event center and murder dozens of people," retorted Boyle.

"He was just a kid," said Kevin, "a geeky, history loving kid. He wasn't capable of doing something like this. Even if he were alive …"

Furman glared at Newman. He was talking loudly within earshot of the recuperating guests. Regardless of the situation, she didn't want a hysterical mob scene. It was important to project a sense of calmness and control. "Here you go young man," she said as she handed a nervous eight-year-old a bottle of Aqua Monde mineral water. The boy reluctantly unscrewed the cap and took a gulp. He paused for a moment as his eyes wandered to Kevin. Being the focus of the boy's attention unnerved Newman. "Can I help you young man?" he blurted awkwardly.

"I heard you talking," the boy said meekly. "The man in the hall. He came back from the dead to kill us? How can we be safe from him?"

Newman realized he was the recipient of simultaneous scowls from both Newman and Boyle. It was time to take a page out of Furman's book. He let out a sigh, smiled and crouched to his knees. Placing a reassuring arm around the boy he said "don't listen to silly adult talk. I was talking about something else. A movie. It was a little bit like this but all the people got away to safety." The boy looked at him ponderously. He was skeptical but he was willing to believe the lie. "Do you promise?"

Kevin grinned "Absolutely. Aqua Monde is the biggest and best corporation in the whole wide world. We will take care of you. Now drink up your water, and rest up. You need to save your energy as we are all going to be getting out of here very, very soon."

The masquerade had worked. The boy extended the last finger from his right hand in Kevin's direction. The duo exchanged a pinky promise shake before the youngster ran off to find his parents. Crisis averted, Kevin resumed the serious discussion in a much quieter tone of voice. "What are we going to do Jim?"
"I have set up a satellite conference with New York in 45 minutes. We will have to take it in the science lab. It's more secure than the boardroom and gives us the privacy we lack here."
"A call with the board of directors?" asked Furman.
"Yes," replied Boyle "but this has become a security issue too. Although we are in international waters this is being treated as a terrorist incident involving U.S. corporate and domestic interests. The Department of Homeland Security and the Pentagon are now involved. They will be the ones calling the shots."

Back in his science lab, Pargiter was furiously pouring bottles of water into a large glass bowl. He was supposed to have attended the opening ceremony but his work had kept him otherwise engaged. On his desk, sat a brick size chunk of ice. He had heated it and watched it melt only to see it reform as a solid, time after time. Electrolysis failed to uncover any impurities in the ice. To all intents, it was pure H_2O but it wasn't behaving as such.

The lab door opened and Dr. Hewlett burst into the room. "Can I help you?" Pargiter was perturbed. He had just poured the last of his 20 water bottles into the glass tank. It was time for him to conduct his experiment. He was not in the mood for visitors.
"Have you seen what is going on out there?" snapped Hewlett indignantly.
"Yes," he replied calmly. "Security asked me to review the video footage. Very strange."
Hewlett approached his workspace. Beside the large tank sat a small glass bowl. A single goldfish was peacefully gliding back and forth in the rounded vessel.

"So we have a crisis on our hands and you're playing with goldfish?" Hewlett was unimpressed.
"Not playing," retorted Pargiter "researching."

He gently lowered his hand into the goldfish bowl and slowly wrapped his hands around the orange occupant. He cupped his other hand over the tiny animal and retrieved it from the bowl. He turned to Hewlett glumly. "You know I am rather fond of this goldfish. But, there are people dying out there so I am afraid he will have to make the ultimate sacrifice." Hewlett was puzzled. Pargiter lowered his hands to the tank full of mineral water. With his fingers just above the surface, he let go of the fish and it plopped into the tank. Having recovered from the shock of the bowl switch, the fish began to eagerly explore its new home.

"Look," demanded Hewlett "I need your help. I am a physician, not a chemist or biologist but there is something very strange going on here."
Pargiter sat up straight and finally gave her his full attention. "Go on," he said.
"The young man in the auditorium. I examined him earlier. He had no vital signs, He was in my professional opinion deceased."
Pargiter nodded. He had heard the same information from the security guards.
"When I was in medical school," Hewlett continued "I read a case study about Tetrodotoxin. A man in Japan was exposed to it after eating an improperly prepared puffer fish. The toxins didn't kill him but he was in a paralytic state where he appeared to be dead for two days. Eventually, he came around in the morgue."
"I have heard similar stories too," replied Pargiter.
"Well, the young man from Norway. According to the guards, the last time anyone saw him alive he had been given a glass of water. Then yesterday we had an old man drop dead. It appeared that he died from asphyxiation with an ice cube lodged in his throat. But the tour guide insisted the old man had no ice in his drink. He did though drink mineral water. Just like the Norwegian. I am wondering if there is a toxin in it. This place is pretty isolated. The aquifers had been untouched for millenia. Who knows if pufferfish or some other marine life may have left toxic traces in there?"

Pargiter was impressed with Hewlett's guesswork. "I like it," he said "it is a very good theory … but completely wrong."
Hewlett rolled her and eyes and let out a harsh sigh.
"I thought the same thing myself," Pargiter continued "but I have tested this water a dozen different ways and found no trace of any kind of impurity. If anything, this Aqua Monde mineral water is cleaner than water you will find anywhere else in the world."
"So if it's not the water," Hewlett mused "perhaps there is some other environmental factor. The volcanic emissions perhaps?"
"Aha" yelped Pargiter excitedly "but you see, it is the water!"

Hewlett was confused. She wasn't sure if Pargiter was a brilliant scientist who talked in riddles or a madman just blurting out words.
"Look at this ice," Pargiter gestured to the block on his counter.
Hewlett reached towards it but Pargiter grabbed her wrist.
"I wouldn't touch it if I were you. While it looks like and is, frozen water. It could also be very dangerous."
"How so?" asked Hewlett.
"For one thing," said Pargiter "it has been resting there on that sheet of blotting paper for the past two hours. It is 78 degrees in this lab. According to science, it should have started melting almost immediately. It hasn't. There isn't a single drop of water on that paper."

Hewlett skeptically prodded the paper at the base of the ice. To her amazement, it was bone dry. "That doesn't make any sense!" she whispered.
"Neither does the fact that I have melted this ice with hot blasts of energy several times and on each occasion, the water has solidified almost immediately back into a block of ice. You said this old man, he drank water and suffocated as there was a block of ice in his throat. Let's imagine the tour rep was right. He drank water from the same source as this and it froze after ingestion causing him to die."

Pargiter's theory seemed preposterous but in the context of the events of the past few days it made sense. Hewlett felt very uneasy. She tried to recall her actions during the last few days and remember if she had drunk any mineral water. As far as she could recall, the plumbing disruption had limited her consumption to purified sea water. Her train of thought was broken as her gaze wandered onto the fish tank.

"Look at the fish!" she exclaimed.

Pargiter spun round to see the tiny goldfish perfectly stationary in the center of the tank. Eyes open, fins outstretched, its tale rigid and flat. It sat like a statue defying gravity in the center of the tank. Both of the spectators began to slowly circle the fish tank. Curiously examining the fish from every angle to see if some foreign object was holding it in place.

The tank was empty. The fish was alone yet deathly still. A slight movement from its gills disturbed the water around it. A second more violent movement shook the entire body of the fish. A third pulse-like vibration followed and the entire body of the fish erupted like a star going supernova as tiny fragments of flesh and blood created a cloud of crimson in the fishtank. Pargiter and Hewlett watched silently in horror as the bloody residue rose to the surface. Through the murky water, something was glinting under the laboratory's harsh light. The grey water became clearer and clearer as particles rose to the surface. As the last of the animal matter dissipated, Hewlett let out an audible yelp. Hovering in the center of the tank, was a crystal clear, exact clone of the fish. The living creature had been replaced by a self-generated ice based replica.

Flomo, Anne and the journalistic duo had been cowering behind the upper deck balcony for several minutes. On the floor below, the zombie-like figure of Henrik had been joined by another similarly ice bound compadre. Padraig was furiously scribbling notes for his next major article. Danny was surreptitiously taking photos of the frozen fiends while trying to avoid capturing their attention.

The resurrection of Henrik had provided an additional complication for Flomo and Anne. Flomo had returned to Aqua Monde with the intention of exposing details about AM Corp's exploitation of Africa. Anne wanted to document the destruction of the archaeological site. Padraig was their best bet for exposing both stories but he was more concerned with the Henrik situation.

"I have an idea," Said Flomo.
"Go ahead," Padraig replied half-interestedly as he finished scribbling notes on his pocket-sized pad.
"See those pipes running along the edge of the railings?" Flomo gestured to a trio of metallic pipes that emerged from the floor at the top of the escalator and followed the balcony before disappearing down the corridor.
"They are carrying high voltage electrical cables. I was on the maintenance crew clearing this place up when we installed them. They are connected to a backup generator that supplies the water plant in the event of a power outage."
"How does that help us?" Anne asked.
"The generator is behind a panel across the hallway," Flomo explained.
"We could use that power source to take out these guys. We lure them onto the metal escalator and boom!"
Padraig was unconvinced. "Bullets didn't affect Henrik. How are you so sure that electricity will?"
"I am not" replied Flomo "But information about AM, her dig site, and the boat that is our only way out of here are all located downstairs on the other side of these two guys. If we try my plan at least we have a shot at getting past them."

It was a risky plan but the silence of the group indicated to Flomo that there were no better options. He pulled a Swiss knife from his pocket and began prying the pipes away from the wall. As the first pipe broke free, the electrical casing at the base of the elevator snapped loose exposing a thick wad of differently colored cords. Flomo tugged violently on the cords until a dozen or so wires snapped somewhere beneath the floor. He thumped his fist against the emergency stop button at the top of the escalator. The metallic staircase ground to a halt.

As Henrik mindlessly paced below, Flomo carefully weaved the ragged electrical cord into the crevasses on the top step. Satisfied with his handiwork, Flomo dashed across the hallway and used his knife to pry the electrical panel off the wall. Behind the panel was a large red notice "Danger high voltage DC current." A stainless steel lever was resting in the "off" off position beneath the sign.
"Wait," cried Padraig "before you do that, what's the plan?" Flomo growled impatiently. "You call them over," he snapped. "Once they hit the stairs I pull the lever. If it works, I flip the power off, we rush past them and get the Hell out of here."

Padraig's right eye began to twitch as he became visibly anxious. "Well," he muttered "when we go down I would suggest we all hold our breath. We don't know if Henrik has been poisoned or something. When we fry him the poison may go airborne."
Flomo smiled and gave Padraig the thumbs up "show time."
Anne jumped to her feet and ran to the top of the escalator. "Henrik! Henrik" she yelled "come on up. We are over here." The Norwegian stopped walking in circles and turned his head in the direction of the escalator. Danny and Padraig joined Anne whose screams were ever more shrill. Henrik and the reanimated security guard slowly made their way towards the escalator. With a loud clunk, Henrik put his boot onto the first step. The encouragement continued from above. "Come on Henrik, it's Anne, come on hurry!"

Slowly and deliberately Henrik made his way up the stairs. As he reached the halfway point, the security guard finally stepped onto the first stair. "Light them up!" Danny cried. With one forceful pull, Flomo switched the power on. Sparks and began to spew from the cord ends attached to the top of the staircase. Henrik and the security guard continued their slow climb.
"It's not working!" cried Anne.
"Wait, look," said Danny. Henrik and the security guard had suddenly stopped in their tracks. First the Norwegian, then the guard below began to shudder violently. Like rag dolls, their limp bodies swayed from side to side buffeting the escalator's handrails. Their feet glued to the stairs by the electrical current. The smell of burning rubber began to waft up the escalator. A small plume of smoke

appeared at the base of Henrik's jeans. Within seconds a small burning cinder on his stitching had evolved into a raging torrent of flame. It raced up his jeans and his battered shirt erupted in fire. Blacked flakes of charred skin began to float from his glowing corpse. Moments later, the security guard was ignited and engulfed in a second ball of flames.

Flomo pushed the lever up to cut the power source. Danny raced to the top of the escalator. As his booted toes touched the metallic stair, a surge of power raced up his leg and flung him back onto the balcony.
"It's still alive" exclaimed Anne.
"Give it a second" Flomo retorted.
Padraig rushed over to Danny's side. His friend was conscious but visibly in pain, lying flat on his back with his head against the wall. The impact of hitting the wall had created a large gash on his scalp. Blood trickled down his forehead and either side of his nose down onto his cheeks.
"Can you stand?" asked Padraig.
"Yeah," said Danny unconvincingly as he gingerly rose to his feet.

"Let's go," Flomo commanded. He rushed past the rest of the group and made his way down the now inactive escalator. He carefully backed away from each of the human candles as he dashed down the now stationery stairs. Anne quickly followed, with her shirt pulled up over her mouth to shield her from the rapidly expanding cloud of fumes and steam. Padraig slowly made his way down the stairs. Danny hobbled along behind him. Padraig wanted to stay close in case Danny lost his balance. The duo clumsily slipped by Henrik without making contact. Just four steps to go. The flaming skeletal remains of the security guard wobbled as Padraig slipped past. With a crack, the unfortunate guard's right fibula and tibia snapped causing the lopsided human inferno to sway to the left directly into the path of Danny.

Danny shrieked as the skull of the guard smacked into his chin. As it did so, a thick cloud of fumes engulfed Danny's upper body. He began to violently. Two steps below Padraig thrust his right arm towards Danny. grabbing a wad of his shirt, Padraig dragged the

hapless photographer down the last few steps.
Danny regained his balance before hunching over and vomiting onto the floor.
"Are you OK?" asked Padraig. Danny still hunched over offered a grunt as his reply.
Flomo was less concerned with his well being "we have to go."

Danny gripped Padraig's arm for support as he straightened up. A nod in the direction of Flomo signaled that Danny was ready to roll. Without a word, the quartet hastily made their way across the lobby. They reached the glass door leading to the guest accommodations. It slid open without prompting. As Flomo stepped through Anne let out a loud scream. "Look!" she cried. The three men turned in the direction of the escalator. The guard's remains had disintegrated into a flaming heap. Further up the stairs, smoke billowed from the scorched remains of Henrik's clothes. On the next stair stood a figure. Tall, angular, and entirely made of ice. It was reminiscent of the figures Anne had seen in the cave paintings. The "water god" as Kenny had called it. The ancient myth recorded in a cave painting was now standing just yards away. Stunned silence gripped the onlookers. Padraig finally broke the silence "Let's run"

Outside the flooded caves, Prince Faisal had slowly trundled past the security guards and stood amidst the tour group. His shirt was saturated with thick globular blood. A huge entry wound exposed the innards of his chest. Patel edged towards him. Edith followed close behind. As he peered more closely, Patel gestured towards the Arabian prince's eyes. Edith looked over. To her horror. His eye sockets were filled with transparent icy balls where his eyes once sat. "He is like the guy from the hall!" she whispered nervously. Gaunt, standing a good distance away had already made the same determination. The trigger-happy security guards were only too willing to hear his theory. With very little encouragement they embraced the notion that Faisal like Henrik was a clear and present threat.

"Back up!" yelled a guard. Patel and Edith stepped away from Faisal as the guard lunged forward. From just inches away, he blasted his rifle into the back of the prince's head. An explosion of blood and bone fragments rained down on the would-be assassin but the Prince remained standing.

Patel was appalled. "You can't hurt them with bullets," he admonished the guard. Rushing forward he snatched the rifle from the flabbergasted guard's hands.
Fearing for her safety, Edith inched away. As she did so, scalding water splashed her achilles. She had unwittingly wandered onto a thin stretch of firm ground between two thinly crusted pools of volcanic discharges. Realizing her situation she glanced at Patel. He quickly grasped her predicament and scanned the ground behind her. The rock narrowed but there was enough space for her to edge back a few feet.
"Edge back," he said calmly "one foot at a time"

Edith put her faith in him and stretched her left foot blindly behind her. After what seemed like an eternity, her toes finally made contact with firm ground. Emboldened, she took another step and another until she could feel the warmth of the volcanic spew steaming onto her calves. "Hey Prince," she yelled, "come towards me."
"What is she doing?" cried Gita. Mike realized her plan. "Quiet Gita, she knows what she is doing."
"Come here Prince, come and get me."

The partially headless husk began to edge towards Edith. Step by step his feet came closer and closer to the volcanic crust. Suddenly, just millimeters from the crust, he stopped. Whatever force controlled the late Prince, seemed to have sufficient awareness to stop in the face of danger.

"Enough of this," roared Patel. He slid his hands to the barrel end of the gun he had requisitioned. He pranced forward, almost skipping and slammed the butt of the gun into the Prince's back. The frozen Arabian wobbled but he stretched his arms to regain his balance. Like Patel, Bradshaw had seen enough. With a single motion, he dove headlong into the bag of the Prince's knees. The staggering figure tipped forward and burst through the flaky crust. A mass of boiling bubbles erupted from the Earth as the fiendish figure slowly sank into oblivion.

A blast of steam left Billy red faced as he lay face down on the ground. As the steam dispersed, he felt a friendly hand grab his shoulder. It was Patel. The Indian helped the Londoner to his feet. "I tried to hit him for six," joked Patel "I was a pretty good cricketer back in Calcutta."

"No mate," replied Billy "someone like that, you can't beat a good old rugby tackle." Pounding his chest excitedly Billy boasted "Harlequins under-13 national rugby champion 1998."

"Well ladies and gents," piped in Gaunt as he made his way forward having been cowering in the rear. "I am glad to see that my plan worked. You're welcome."

Shaking heads, eye rolls and sighs quickly wiped the smile off his face.

"Look at this," Patel said excitedly. The bullet the guard had fired was resting at his feet. He bent down and picked it up. "It is covered in ice. His eyes were like glass, maybe his body was somehow frozen?"

"Now we have had our fun," interrupted Edith "let's go and find that boat."

ENDURANCE

After witnessing the emergence of the ice figure. Padraig had convinced his group to head to the science center. Perhaps, Dr. Pargiter could shed some light on the situation. If not, he at least had plenty of equipment that they could turn into weapons.

As they neared the science lab, an elevator came to rest in the hallway behind them. With the typical "ding" the doors slid open. Boyle and Furman emerged. Enraged at the site of the duo, Flomo charged at Boyle. Gripping his fingers tightly around his neck, he slammed him into the wall. Stunned, Boyle tried to back away, but Flomo struck him in the face with a powerful left hook. He lined up a follow-up blow before Padraig and Anne grabbed his arms and restrained him.

"You son of a bitch!" Flomo cried "you're killing people. Sucking Africa dry to run this sham operation." Boyle wiped a trickle of blood from beneath his nose.
"Deny it! Deny it!" roared Flomo.
"So," said Boyle "you're the Liberian who poisoned our water supply. I imagine you're behind the massacre we just saw?"
"Don't be an idiot" snapped Anne "that was something else. Something outside science."
Boyle shrugged. "Well that is as may be," he said "but this place? Yeah, we borrowed some water from Liberia. So what? You didn't even have a functioning water system until we invested in Monrovia. Contaminated water, no water, what is the difference?"

Padraig was disgusted. "The difference?" he said, "the difference is that you are getting tax breaks and money from the UN for helping resolve a water shortage while in fact, you are profiteering from creating one."
"Not true," Boyle retorted, "we had good intentions. But we couldn't extract water here as quickly as our investors demanded. This place wouldn't exist without the investors so we had to act. Once this place is operating fully we will be sending plenty of water to Liberia, to Ivory Coast, Niger and any other country that wants it."
"Lies!" yelled Flomo. "I have read the research. I used to be a broker and I still have connections. You got the Liberian government to fund this whole operation by issuing bonds. The bonds are contingent on your profits, but the Liberian taxpayers are on the hook if this place fails."
"That my friend," said Boyle "is a risk they were willing to take. Regardless, the plan was to make a profit so taxpayers wouldn't be on the hook."
"If that were so," continued Flomo "what about the credit default swap."

Boyle was silent. He looked at Furman shame-faced. She let out a disappointed sigh. Anne was perplexed "Can someone explain to me what you're talking about."
Furman explained that a credit default swap is similar to an insurance contract. Investors use the devices to insure high-risk ventures that traditional insurance firms won't touch.

Satisfied with her explanation, Flomo moved onto the next stage of his allegations.

"After the civil war, nobody wanted to invest in Liberia. The bonds for Aqua Monde were high yield. Anyone foolish enough to buy one would earn annual premiums of 25 or 30 percent. The higher the risk, the higher the rewards. After Prince Faisal's investment, internal reports showed that the project was unviable. Aqua Monde diverted cash from the project and started buying up billions of dollars on credit default swaps. The swaps were attached to Liberian government debt. If the government defaults on the bonds, the swap holders get paid trillions in compensation. When AM stopped investing in the island, the risk of failure became a certainty. It was just a matter of waiting for the whole thing to go belly up. Leaving Liberia bankrupt, creating an artificial drought, and Boyle and the other executives could cash in their chips and each walk away with hundreds of billions."

"Jim" demanded Furman "is this true."

Boyle shrugged "what difference does it make now? this place is finished anyway."

"You son of a bitch," Furman slapped Boyle across the cheek.

"You destroyed the priceless artifacts to build a swimming pool for a water park that will never be built," Anne followed her outburst by slapping Boyle's other cheek. The businessman smirked and shook his head. "My friend is dead because of you." All the emotion she had repressed in order to survive, suddenly erupted. Tears began to flow down her reddened cheeks. She turned and buried her face into Flomo's chest. He placed a comforting arm around her back.

Padraig stood awkwardly beside them wondering how Flomo had climbed above him in Anne's pecking order. Boyle felt equally uncomfortable. He attempted to change the subject. "How about you?" he asked "Padraig, do you have some grievance against me too?" Padraig shook his head.

"Well on a personal level, I lost my job because your corrupt corporation paid off the media to keep silent about your antics. But relative to the archaeological destruction, financial fraud, third world exploitation, and widespread bloodshed, I guess I got off easy."

Boyle laughed as he regained his composure. "Well, whatever you may all think of me. I have to be on a satellite conference in fifteen minutes. The people on the other end of the line offer us our best … or only chance of getting out of here alive. So unless anyone else wants to assault me, I suggest we make our way into the science lab."

There were no objections as Boyle entered a six digit code to open the laboratory door. The emotional quintet entered the room. Inside, Dr. Pargiter and Dr. Hewlett were huddled around a fish tank. A large screen topped with a miniature camera was now set up on Pargiter' desk.

"Ah, we have visitors," said Pargiter excitedly.
"It is not a social visit," said Boyle " we are here for the satellite conference and to see if you have come up with anything."
"Nice to see you too," said Pargiter sarcastically "we have made some progress but first let me ask you a few questions. The killer, the security guards indicated that he was firing ice pellets. Did anyone get a good look at him?"
"We did," said Anne "He was one of my friends. We just saw him on the way here but he wasn't firing ice pellets, he was ice. It was like he was an ice humanoid trapped in Henrik's body."
"Very good," said Pargiter. "well the ice is key or rather the water. The Aqua Monde spring water to be precise."
"Go on," instructed Boyle.
"Are any of you familiar with dark energy?" Pargiter was met with a lot of blank faces before Danny piped up. "Isn't that a type of matter from a different dimension. I saw something about it on Ancient Aliens."
Pargiter chuckled. "Not exactly. It is a force that doesn't follow the natural laws of physics. It is from the realm of what we call 'quantum physics.' Dark matter defies gravity and causes the universe to expand. We cannot see it. We cannot quantify it but quantum physics tells us that it must exist."
"So you think this is what we have here?" asked Padraig.
"No," said Pargiter "but something similarly odd, that defies the laws of physics. I assume you are all familiar with the concept of an avatar. A deity, or force from elsewhere manifesting itself in a physical form on Earth."

Everyone cautiously nodded to acknowledge a level of understanding.

"Well that is exactly what we have here," continued Pargiter "only this avatar only manifests itself through the H20 found in the aquifers on this island. It can control the water in another organism, a fish, a human, and use its body as an avatar. Or, it can create a mold from a physical form, then break out as a crystalline ice replica that can move about as an organism in its' own right. It can self regulate its temperature. It can rapidly turn water into ice or steam regardless of the outside environment."

"And it is malevolent?" asked Padraig.

"Not necessarily," Pargiter replied. "We have no physical trace of its brain or its operating system. It may be malevolent, intent on killing us all. On the other hand, it may be amoral. Incapable of rational thought and purely instinctive, killing people it can use as hosts, or individuals it perceives to be obstacles or a threat."

"This is absurd," ridiculed Boyle.

"I would have agreed with you a few hours ago," retorted Hewlett "but I saw for myself, a goldfish obliterated by the water, only to be replaced by a frozen duplicate."

Anne had always felt archaeology was undervalued but the conversation suddenly empowered her. "This thing has been here before," she said "the cave paintings. They featured an ice figure, it grew in each section until in the last picture, it looked as if all the people were washed away in some kind of flood."

Boyle shook his head "this doesn't make any sense. If this water creature is so resourceful and deadly, how come no one has ever encountered it before … in recorded history."

"This island was completely isolated for eons," said Anne "if it is based in the water here, then no one would have been exposed to it since the settlers here moved or were wiped out thousands of years ago. It was lying dormant underground until you started drilling here."

Flomo had been listening to the conversation intently. He wasn't sure if his thoughts would be dismissed but he decided to share his own insights.

"Where I grew up," he said "there was a tradition about a spirit called Mami Wata. She lived in water, and was made of water. She would appear in springs, lakes, rivers. She could be capable of good or evil. People blamed her for floods and droughts. There has been a resurgence in that tradition since Aqua Monde showed up in town. I know it's just a stupid fairytale for kids but, I don't know. Maybe somehow there's a connection." Boyle scoffed. Pargiter gave the executive a stern look before turning back to Flomo.

"All of us," said Pargiter softly, "rationalize the unexplained by interpreting it in terms that we understand. I am a scientist so I look for a scientific explanation. Other people look to traditions and superstitions. Maybe we are both right, maybe we are both wrong. At this point, it is all conjecture. For the time being, your community's superstitions are just as valid as my hypotheses. They are all just theories." Flomo smiled. He didn't believe the superstitions but he did have deep respect for his country and his ancestors. He welcomed the fact that Pargiter at least was speaking about his homeland in positive terms.

Boyle shook his head frustratedly. "All this talk of dark energy, water imps and what not. Bottom line is that we are in danger here. There must be some kind of way we can defeat these …. things."
"We didn't defeat them," said Padraig "but we, I mean Flomo, found a way to slow them down. He electrified an escalator." As he spoke he noticed the melancholy look on Anne's face. She was obviously disturbed by the reminder of Hernik's demise. After a slight hesitation, Padraig continued. "It was pretty gruesome … but they were disabled for a while. Then the ice creature seemed to break out."

"Electricity?" asked Pargiter rhetorically "very ingenious. The DC current would have broken down some of the water into pure carbon and oxygen. Sadly, these things have the ability to reintegrate their component parts. Electrocution isn't a permanent solution but it can buy you some time."

Furman gasped. She had been thinking about Henrik consuming the water when her thoughts floated back to the room from which she came.

"You say the water carries this ... entity?" she asked of Pargiter. He nodded.
"We spent the last few hours trying to calm down survivors in the ballroom. The Norwegian was between us and the kitchens. The only provisions we had were bottled water. We handed them to everyone. Then we locked them in."

The blood rushed from Boyle's face as a tingling shiver rolled from his neck down his spine. He pushed Pargiter to the side and grabbed the mouse for his laptop. He frantically entered the passcode to the security system software. A dozen squares containing live video popped up on screen. He moved his mouse over the one in the bottom left corner. With a double-click, the video expanded to fill the whole screen. To everyone's horror, the ballroom looked like a plowed field. Bodies, on top of bodies, stationary, lifeless, and blood-stained. A flicker of movement in the corner of the room caught Boyle's attention. He double clicked the area on screen. The camera zoomed in.

A cuboid, transparent figure filled the monitor. Boyle staggered back then sunk to his knees. He remembered the child. The boy Kevin had spoken to. The youngster who was told, and believed, that the corporation would rescue everyone. A helpless, hopeful child excited about his first trip overseas. Now he was dead. Slain by unknown forces Boyle had helped unleashed this greed fuelled scheme. No one looked at Boyle. No one said a word. Each of them quietly felt their own sense of grief. Their petty career ambitions seemed much less important than before. Preserving antiquities, writing articles, fighting or creating corporate greed. None of these mattered when compared with mass slaughter. The period of introspection ended as Flomo made the sign of the cross.

"I need to leave," said Danny as the silence was shattered.
"What do you mean 'leave'?" Asked Padraig aggressively "we all want to leave this God-forsaken place!"
"You don't understand," Danny continued somberly. "I am contaminated. When the old man died I picked up that ice cube."
"That was a long time ago," snapped Padraig dismissively "you would have died by now!"

Danny shook his head. "On the escalator, I gashed my head. On the way down, I got caught up with that thing. I inhaled a lot of fumes. This thing spreads as water, so I imagine water vapor would have the same effect. But not only that, the guard was melting, a bunch of water sprayed my face and across the back of the head. With the open wound, it is just a matter of time. I need to leave so I don't endanger the group."

Padraig was exasperated. He couldn't process any more death and destruction in one day. He convinced himself Danny was being dramatic, foolhardy even.
"What do you propose to do? Lock yourself out there and just hang around to die? That's idiotic!"
Danny's mind was made up.
" I hate to say this," ventured Pargiter "but he is probably right."
"What do you know?" Padraig was indignant "you've been hidden away in here the whole time playing with your goldfish. You don't know anything. You said it yourself. Your ideas are no better than folklore."
"Padraig stop," urged Anne.
"No. Don't listen to them, Danny. This is stupid," Padraig's eyes reddened and his voice quivered as he became more emotional.
"Good luck Danny," said Flomo. He extended his hand. Danny chuckled and Flomo withdrew it realizing the perils of contact.
"I am sorry," said Furman.
"You are very brave," Anne whispered as a single tear meandered down her cheek.
"Goodbye Padraig," Danny said before turning and making his way to the door.
"Don't be an idiot!" Padraig's cry faded into the distance as Danny forcefully made his exit down the corridor.

COMEUPPANCE

"Have you seen this crap?" Senator Clark barked across the boardroom table. The Kansas ranking member of the Homeland defense committee was immersed in a live broadcast on TV. He sunk his bald head into his hands as the TV report continued. Onscreen, a caption read 'Claudia Porcelli, Knox Media'. Padraig's boss was being interviewed live on a rival network. Clark's guests seated themselves at the table and began to watch the newscast. They were all male. General Santos, a rotund, middle-aged man with two rows of medals on his lapel, sat directly opposite Clark. CIA Director Tim Tucker, a wispy septuagenarian sat to the general's left. Securities and Exchange Commission Chairman Mike Moldovan, bushy-eyebrowed with a mop of dark hair, sat beside Tucker. Two jittery looking executives from Aqua Monde Corp; a tall thin man and a shorter heavy-set fellow, sat on the other side of the desk. Clark had remarked that they looked like 'Laurel and Hardy' upon their arrival. Their inept corporate practices only served to strengthen that connection.

Clark used his remote to turn up the volume. "The whole thing is a scam, a huge Ponzi scheme," said the onscreen journalist. "AM Corp. knew they couldn't generate enough water from this site so they had the Liberian government --- one of the poorest in the world -- fund the upfront costs with a promise of lavish returns. The tankers they claimed were bringing clean water to Africa, were actually draining Monrovian reservoirs to fill spas for guests on the artificial island."

Clark abruptly hit the off switch and slammed the controller on the table.
"We have midterms coming up. Now to add to terrorism in the Mid-Atlantic we have another example of Wall Street running riot. You sons of bitches are finished. I am telling you." SEC Chairman Mike Moldovar made a loud 'tut' sound and shook his head in disapproval at the AM executives.
"I don't know why you're acting the innocent," Clark scolded him "you're asleep at the wheel if your regulators have to learn about this scandal from watching cable TV."
Moldovan, slunk back into his seat, he bowed.

"The securities stuff will have to wait," said Clark. "More immediately our concern is the security situation. You have all seen the emails and video files that a Dr. Pargiter forwarded to AM Corp. Terrifying stuff. Now tell me, had your company ever encountered anything like this before? Bear in mind, you're already in serious trouble so I strongly urge you to offer an unabridged version of the facts."

The two executives from AM exchanged glances before responding to their questioner with muted frowns. "Nothing," Clark continued "No issues with water freezing, no mysterious deaths, no glass looking humanoids?"
"Well," ventured the Oliver Hardy look-alike "there had been

problems with water freezing. That is why we ended up getting water from overseas. That is where the Liberia supply came in. But none of this other stuff."

Clark turned to CIA Director Tucker. "The President has been informed of all this?"
"Yes senator," Tucker replied "but we need to clear the room before we can have those discussions. Myself, you and the general are the only ones with appropriate security clearance."
"Hold on a second," complained the Stan Laurel executive "We were the ones who gave you this information. It is our project. It isn't in the US. How can you say we aren't qualified to be involved in these discussions?" Clark was enraged.
"The island is yours, the protection of US assets and persons is a federal matter. Moreover, the response to this crisis is not your concern. Whose dumbass idea was it to play God and build land in the middle of the ocean? You can't fight nature. The whole concept was ludicrous even from the outset. You guys have built yourselves a modern day Tower of Babel. We are now waiting to see when Babel comes crashing down."
"Or when Babel floods Senator," quipped Director Tucker.
"I don't appreciate your dark humor Director," Clark replied, "and I hope for all our sakes that when Babel does flood, the contaminated inhabitants don't flee to every corner of the Earth."

There was a stunned silence as everyone silently pondered the options for containing the crisis. None of the resolutions were palatable. "It is now a critical security matter," Clark continued. He glared at the nervous executives. "You have to leave," commanded Tucker.
"You heard the man," barked Clark "get the hell out of here, you too Moldovan. Go and figure out what it is your agents do all day when they should be preventing corporate fraud."

The admonished trio quickly rose from their seats and exited the room. Clark allowed time for them to disperse further down the hallway before resuming the discussion.
"So what are we thinking? Islamic Terrorists?" he asked Tucker.
"No Senator," Tucker replied.

"What then? The Russians?" Clark's second guess was marginally better but Tucker shook his head. General Santos disagreed. "With respect Director, you know and I know that the Russians have spent billions on various types of psychokinetic weapons, alternative energies, telepathy studies and so on. This ability to remotely control a substance, be it water or ice, seems exactly like the kind of thing the KGB would dream up."
Tucker laughed "We can all dream General but the reality is something else."
Clark was intrigued by Santos' comments. "Hold on Ted, don't just blow it off. These things that Santos is talking about. Why are you so sure there is no credence to them?"

Ted took a deep breath. He felt he should only share information when absolutely necessary. Nonetheless, he realized his inquisitors would not accept his silence.
"I know," he said "because one of our assets is running Koschei. It is a secret FSB program named after a Russian fairytale. It is designed to research and weaponize non-material things: dark energy, antimatter, telekinesis and so on.
It has been around since the last days of the KGB in the eighties. Despite heavy investment, their research has yielded very little. They claim they used wave frequencies, Gamma, Delta and so on, to ignite the Romanian revolution in 1989. One unit made a lot of money rigging poker games in Monte Carlo. They used the money to fund counter-revolutionary activities in Central America. Supposedly, telepathy played a part, but there is no hard evidence to back that up. So no gentlemen, the Russians do not have the know-how to pull this off. In fact, the only thing related to Russia that bears any resemblance to this was an incident in 1982. The Russians didn't instigate it, they were on the receiving end."
"What happened in 1982?" asked Clark.
"Seven divers, the Navy's top men, were doing training drills for arctic activities. They explored a lake in Siberia. It had only recently become accessible as the permafrost began to thaw. The lake, we believe, had been under thick layers of ice for thousands of years."
"And what happened?" asked Clark impatiently.
"Seven divers went down, four came up. Two were critically injured and died within hours. The surviving two reported that their

colleagues had been attacked by some kind of aquatic humanoids. Large beings, in the water that seemed to be made of liquid. I guess kind of like ghosts if you believe in that kind of thing. There was a faint body shape to them so they could be distinguished from the lake water. These things attacked the divers, disconnected their breathing apparatus. Clearly, they were somewhat intelligent, and hostile."

"What did you Russians do about it?" asked Clark.

"Officially?" teased Tucker "nothing. Unofficially, they sent down some armed submersibles and the crews never made it out alive. They eventually sealed off the area and began to use it as a test site for strategic nuclear weapons. My guess? They nuked the area so they could entomb these things for another 1,000 years."

"Should we follow suit?" asked Clark somberly.

"I can think of worse ideas," said Tucker.

"Respectfully, I disagree," said Santos. "We could be onto something here that offers great opportunities for our military. We shouldn't just blow this place off the map. Or if we do, we need to at least get a sample of this water. This guy Pargiter down there. He is a clean water specialist. He doesn't have the tools and research we have here. This may be a mystery to him but if we get it to Groom Lake then who knows what our people could learn?"

"He has a point," said Tucker.

"Yeah," said Clark pensively "we have some big decisions to make, and quickly"

Edith's tour group had carefully navigated most of the resort without encountering any danger. They made their way through the eerily dark casino, past the kids' amusement area, into the registration

zone. No one was at the front desk. No one was anywhere. It was like a ghost town until a figure appeared at the other end of the foyer. A man wearing a black leather jacket. He was slowly wandering about although unlike Hernik, he seemed to be in control of his faculties. As he came closer, Edith recognized him.
"Danny!" she yelled. He stopped and glanced around until he saw the tour representative and her group lurking in the shadows. Without reply, Danny made an abrupt about-turn and started to head for the exit.
"Stop! Danny wait," Edith cried "It's me. Edith," she raced after him. He was doing his best to ignore her but as she rapidly gained ground, he stopped and turned to face her.
Edith grinned broadly from ear to ear. "Thank God you are OK. I was so worried about you."
"I can't talk to you," Danny muttered curtly.
"What do you mean? Why are you trying to run away? I thought we were friends," Edith said sadly.
"I am dangerous," Danny blurted.
"Dangerous? I don't understand."
"It is the water," said Danny "we were in the science lab. They figured out there is something wrong with the water here. It kills people. It turns people into killers."

Edith was puzzled "The water? but we have all been drinking water. We are OK."
"No," said Danny, "it is the volcanic water. The drinking water from taps, pool water, it is all either desalinated or exported from overseas. The bad water is the water from the island. The bottled drinking water from AM."
Edith thought back to the pool incident. "Mr. Pompidou drank that."
"Yes," said Danny "so did Henrik, some of the guards. Everyone who is dead or possessed by this weird water borne entity. Everyone except me."
"You drank it?" asked Edith nervously.
"I inhaled the steam, the water sept into my open wounds. I have been exposed. It is just a matter of time before I become like them."
"Can't they fix you?" Edith reasoned "these scientists? Can't they make you better?"
"No," said Danny dryly "they don't understand it any more than we

do. It's some kind of lifeform. It uses the water as an avatar. No one knows how to stop it."

"But, what are you going to do? You can't just stay here all alone."

"I have to," said Danny sadly "if I don't, I will put you and everyone else at risk. You have to stay away from me."

"I care about you," Edith whispered softly.

"You have other people to worry about. I will be OK. I have no job, no home, no family to go back to. This place is as good as any for me."

"Well," Edith replied, "when you put it like that, I don't have much to live for either."

"Yes you do," said Danny "the people in your group. You can lead them out of here. They don't know this place. You are their only hope."

"I can't," said Edith "I can't just leave you!"

Danny shook his head sadly. "Then I will have to leave you."

He turned and sprinted through the exit doors. Within seconds he was out of sight down the long dark corridor. Edith wanted to run after him. She knew it would be futile. If he really was infected, he would run and run till he could harm no one.

"Who was he?" asked Sam. She had quietly encroached on the tail end of the conversation. "He was a friend," said Edith " a good man."

The rest of the tourists had now surrounded her. They were ready for some more directions. "We are very close now to the private docks, it is where the yachts are. Our ticket out of here," Edith said as she feigned optimism.

"Who will drive this vessel for us?" asked the ever quizzical Mike Patel.

"I will," boasted Owen Gaunt, "I have been a boatman all my life."

"I thought you were from Nebraska?" asked Patel.

"I am" Gaunt replied meekly "we have lakes in Nebraska. Small ones, but we have some."

The mood in the science laboratory was tense. It was time for the satellite conference call. Kevin Newman had joined the grieving survivors after an unsuccessful jaunt to locate his missing yacht. He had been shocked to learn about Danny's departure. Not so much the self-sacrifice, as the fact that the water was the key to all of this. Unbeknown to the rest of the group, he had drunk a bottle himself while in the ballroom. He convinced himself he could 'shake it off' but he decided to keep that fact from the others.

The black screen on the monitor suddenly burst to life. Sitting at his desk, was Senator Clark. He wasn't the man Boyle had been expecting to see.
"Good evening," said the Senator.
"Senator Clark?" Boyle recognized him from news shows "I was expecting a call with the board."
"There has been a change of plan," said Clark "things are moving quickly. We received data and video from your chief scientist Pargiter." Boyle peered over his shoulder at the scientist. He had not authorized, nor was he aware of any information sharing. Pargiter smiled glibly. He had lost all faith in his superiors but he hoped someone back home could make good use of his findings.

"We have a team of highly skilled Navy Seals operating in the Mid-Atlantic. They are en route to Aqua Monde. They will take care of the survivors and address any threat to life."
"Good luck with that," muttered Flomo.
"Given the situation, they are aware of the dangers on the island.

Consequently, ensure that none of you are armed when they arrive. Anyone holding a gun, knife or weapon of any kind will be considered an enemy combatant and will be neutralized."
Padraig raised an eyebrow. Flomo shook his head. It was already well established that the ice creatures were impervious to bullets, so why would the survivors need to be disarmed? "I have one other request," Clark continued "To tackle this menace, we need information. Be prepared to hand over a one-liter sample of the Aqua Monde water when the Seals arrive. Good luck, and God Bless America."

As suddenly as it started, the conference was over.
"That was weird," remarked Padraig "no questions, no 'how are holding up?' just 'get us a water sample and drop your guns."
"I imagine it is just standard protocol," suggested Furman.
"I don't like it either," said Flomo.
Anne pouted her lips and addressed the Liberian "I have had a really rough day. I have a glimmer of hope that help is on the way. Don't take that away from me."
Flomo shrugged. "Well, I don't plan to be here when they get here anyway."
"Where are you off to?" asked Pargiter.
"The dock," said Flomo. "You forget, once the dust settles on this, when they have given the executives a slap on the wrist for securities fraud, they are going to want to blame someone. The money behind this will come after me 'the terrorist' who dumped cow's carcasses in the water supply. I don't fancy spending the next 10 years as a prisoner of conscience in Guantanamo Bay."
"I am coming with you," said Boyle.
"You're not exactly my first choice for a crewmate," quipped Flomo.
"I may be a big fish here but in Wall Street I am nobody. The SEC will drop the hammer on people like me when they review the financials. They won't send me to Guantanamo, but Ryker's Island is equally unappealing."
"Where are you going? Liberia?" asked Padraig.
"No, said Flomo "they've got enough problems without harboring fugitives. I quite fancy Brazil. It is only a little further."
"Works for me" Boyle laughed "no extradition treaty."
"Well give my regards to Ronnie Biggs." Padraig's joke was lost on

this audience. "Ronnie Biggs! The great train robber, he ran off to Brazil." The elaboration was of no help. Padraig sighed in frustration.

"Alright," said Flomo "let's go before those troops get here."
Boyle and Flomo exchanged hugs and handshakes with everyone before departing.

Pargiter reached under his desk and produced a one-liter plastic bottle of water. He unscrewed the cap and took a large gulp. "What are you doing? You'll kill yourself" exclaimed Anne. Pargiter chuckled, " this is one I brought from home. Buxton's finest."
He reached under his desk and produced a near identical bottle. The second bottle bore the familiar logo of Aqua Monde. "This is the one the Pentagon is after," stated Pargiter.
"Well just make sure you don't mix them up," said Anne.

DEMOCIDE

'PRIVATE DOCK NO UNAUTHORIZED ACCESS.'

The sign on the door was just another rule that was about to be broken. Edith and her group had been scurrying around hallways for hours. Their final destination was on the other side of the door. No one was around to determine who did and didn't pass for authorized personnel anyway. There was just one problem. The door was locked. Construction work in the docking area had fallen behind schedule. As an interim solution, work crews had installed convention wooden doors with metal grilled portals for viewing access.

"Does anyone have a coat hanger?" asked Gita Patel.
"We could give it a good whack." offered Billy.

"I don't think that would work," said Mike "the door opens in this direction. If we charge it, we will just jam it further into the frame." Edith peered through the porthole. On the far side of the dock was an identical door. She knew it was a good 20-minute walk and in all probability, that door would be locked as well.

"What's that noise?" Ben Bradshaw was the only person not involved in the door examination. Consequently, he was the first to hear a low humming sound emanating from outside. "I hear it too," said Gaunt "It's a buzzing, like an engine or a …"

"Helicopter," Edith finished his sentence. She had visual confirmation to back up the sound. Through the porthole, she could see two black helicopters circling outside the dock. Heavily armed soldiers, equipped with helmets and gas masks were abseiling down to the dock. Upon hitting the ground, the soldiers weaved their way through the unoccupied boats.

"Hey help us!" Edith began thumping the window eager to attract attention. It was to no avail, the soldiers were well out of hearing distance. "What are they doing?" asked Patel as he observed the men pulling black devices from their backpacks, They attached one to each boat. "Some kind of tracking devices?" suggested Sam.

"To track what?" retorted Patel "empty stationary vessels?"

Edith glanced across the dock at the other entry door. Perhaps it was worth running over there. She was about to share the idea when the opposite door swung open. In the doorway, she could see a man in a dark suit. It was Boyle.

Boyle stood in the doorway overlooking the Navy Seals as they swarmed over the boats like workers bees. Flomo stayed out of sight with his back against the wall in the hallway.

"I don't like it," said Flomo "I am not sure they are here to rescue us."

"Nonsense," said Boyle, "America's finest. I am going down there." Flomo gripped Boyle's arms.

"Are you forgetting yourself? Rikers Island? The SEC? What about

Brazil?"
Boyle smiled "I have a good attorney. I will take my chances."
He violently snatched his arm back from Flomo and made his way onto the top level of the dock. He found himself on a metallic c-shaped platform that overlooked the boats. Beneath him were 10 rows of vessels, separated by walkways that provided crew access.

The Navy Seals had finished their work on the boats. Four of them ran outside onto the edge of the dock. Their waiting helicopter lowered a cable and the quartet quickly climbed their way to safety. The other four men crouched underneath the stairwell connecting the dock to the overlook where Boyle was located.
"Hi gentleman, my name is Jim Boyle. I am the" Boyle was in mid-sentence striding towards the top of the stairs when a chain reaction of explosions ripped through the boats. One by one, synchronized like dominos, a huge ball of fire blew a hole in the hull of each and every vessel. As the smoke cleared, Boyle could see lifeboats and masts floating in the shallow water around the scuppered vessels. The four Navy Seals emerged from underneath the stairwell. After admiring their own handiwork, they high-fived one another and began to ascend the stairs. Boyle was waiting for them. Upon seeing him, they raced up the staircase and surrounded him.

Flomo was just feet away waiting anxiously in the hallway. He heard the explosion, he heard the footsteps, now he waited to see what would come next. At another door, 100 yards across the dock, Edith, Billy, and Mike were mystified at the events that were unfolding. "Who are you? Identify yourself?" it was difficult to comprehend the muffled voice of the Seal whose face was obscured by a gas mask. Boyle correctly guessed the nature of the conversation. "My name is Jim Boyle. I am the CEO here. What is going on? Why did you blow up those boats." The lead Seal maneuvered a microphone attached to his helmet so it rested just above the nozzle of his gas mask. "We have one positive ID. Jim Boyle CEO. Over" After waiting for an unhead response, he flicked his right finger forward. The Seal to Boyle's left immediately fired off three rounds straight at Boyle's chest. "One target neutralized."
Flomo had heard enough, he darted down the corridor racing back towards the laboratory. On the other side of the dock, Edith led a

hysterical group charging down the hallway. It was now apparent to everyone. The Seals hadn't come to rescue anyone, they had come to wipe them out.

Flomo flew into the lab, profusely sweating and gasping for air. He almost collided with Anne as he ran towards his fellow survivors.
"What's wrong Flomo," Anne asked, "what happened?"
"The Navy Seals," Flomo exclaimed "they aren't coming to save us. They want to wipe us all out. Destroy the ice creatures, destroy the island, destroy the witnesses."
As Flomo hunched over struggling for breath, Anne looked skeptically at him.
"That doesn't make any sense," she said, "why would you think that?"
Flomo used her arm as a support to pull himself up straight.
"Anne," he reasoned, "listen to me. We were at the dock. They arrived and planted explosives on each and every boat so we would have no way to escape. Boyle went out, he identified himself. They proceeded to shoot him dead at point blank range."
"They think we are all contaminated," said Padraig in horror.
"Where is Cathy? and Kevin?" Flomo asked as his eyes scanned the room.
"They went after you two. They wanted to hitch a ride," said Padraig.
As he finished his sentence, gunshots echoed in the distance.

"They are coming this way" pleaded Flomo "we've got to go."
"There's no way out," explained Padraig "those ice creatures are blocking us that way and we have gun-toting Rambo's coming from the other direction."
Flomo, Anne and Padraig were all gripped by terror but Pargiter was

perfectly calm.
"I have an idea," he said "but you are going to have to trust me."
"OK," said Padraig "as long as it is a good plan."
"Go and hide in my storeroom," Pargiter commanded.
"That is it? That is your great plan?" Padraig cried in exasperation. "These are trained killers, I am pretty sure they will think to look in the closet if we are playing a little game of hide and seek."
"Before they look in there, they will come in here because they are looking for me and they are looking for this," Pargiter waved the bottle of Aqua Monde water in the air.
"And? asked Padraig impatiently.
"And you just leave the rest to me," Pargiter snapped forcefully "now hurry up. They are on their way."

Padraig shook his head. Pargiter's plan or lack thereof seemed like lunacy but the Seals were closing in. There was no other choice. He followed Flomo and Anne into the storeroom, slamming and locking the door behind him. Pargiter remained at his desk with his two bottles of water in front of him. He checked his watch nervously. He could hear doors slamming and footsteps getting louder. He reached down and took a sip of water from the nearest bottle.

The last of the Seals who had climbed out of the dock clambered his way back into the helicopter. He gave the thumbs up to the pilot. Just ahead of their craft was the second copter. Barring the pilot, the crew were still on the island. The two craft slowly moved away from the dock in unison. "Head to zone two to neutralize remaining survivors, over," said the pilot of the empty craft. A large splodge of white fecal matter suddenly blocked his view as what appeared to be a fountain of bird droppings came raining down on his windshield. "Man, what the?"

In the second copter, the pilot chuckled into his radio. "Hey man looks like those seagulls have it in for you." His luck wasn't any better. One bird dropping, then another, and another, and another hit his windshield. Startled, he let go of the controller and the craft started to veer sideways. He fought to control it when he heard a commotion behind him. In the rearview mirror he could see half a dozen seagulls viciously flapping their wings at his colleagues. The aggressive birds had flown in through the open doorway.

"What the hell? get these things out of here," he admonished his colleagues. In response, a flurry of blood, feathers and ice particles came flying over his shoulder. He glanced back only to see two sharp yellow claws slash into his eyeballs.

On the ground below, Edith and her tour group had made their way back to the dig site. It was familiar territory that passed for a safe zone. Spiraling wind created a cloud of dust at their feet as two erratically moving helicopters appeared overhead.

"Not the bloody seagulls again?" exclaimed Billy. The two craft were weaving back and forth, all the while being bombarded by diving seagulls. As the machines' pilots rapidly lost control, the tail rotor of one craft connected with the top rotor of the other. Metal shards were flung in every direction as the two copters plummeted to Earth. With a colossal explosion, they smashed into the Earth, only to sink rapidly through the thin volcanic crust into the boiling toxic water beneath the surface.

AVATAR

Pargiter sat alone in his lab. Head hunched over, hands by his side, he sat silently waiting for his guests to arrive. His wait was over. "Get up, identify yourself?" roared the lead Navy Seal. He stood in the doorway, gun pointed at Pargiter while his three colleagues crept by him and formed a circle around the scientist. Pargiter was unmoved. He made no sound and didn't move a muscle. "I told you to get up." Again Pargiter was unresponsive.
In the neighboring room, Flomo, Padraig and Anne were listening with their ears pressed against the door.

"What is Pargiter playing at?" whispered Padraig.
"I have no idea," replied Anne.
"I think I have," said Flomo.
From behind the locked door, they heard metal chair legs being scraped against the floor as the Seals closed in on Pargiter. "What is wrong with him?" asked a husky-voiced male.
"Aagggggg" came a blood-curdling cry from the same man. A volley of gunshots erupted followed by more screams and squeals. Sparks from gunshots, and the shadows of bodies blocking out the light gave the hidden trio an idea of the action that was unfolding.

Flomo slid the latch on the door and began to turn the handle. Padraig firmly gripped Flomo's knuckles in a vain attempt to stop him. Flomo brushed him aside. He opened the door just a few inches. Immediately he saw one set of bloodied boots laying on the floor. On the far side of the lab, a lifeless soldier was draped over a desk top. Flomo opened the door slightly further. As he did so, he was able to see the aged scientist, arm outstretched, his hand connected to the back of a soldiers head by a jagged blade of ice. "Come on," Flomo said "he has done this for us. He has given us a chance."

He pulled Anne to her feet. They crept through the door and hurried across the lab without giving Pargiter a second look. Padraig took a deep breath of air and ran across the lab. As he neared the exit, he slipped on some blood and struck his knee on a chair. The collision made a loud clanking sound that caught Pargiter's attention. Padraig, paralyzed by fear stopped in his tracks and exchanged eye contact with the scientist. He looked the same as before, only the familiar wise old blue eyes had been replaced by empty transparent shells. As he pondered Padraig, the ice blade he had rammed in the soldier's throat began to expand in both directions. With a slight clipping sound, it ruptured the skin on the perimeter of his throat. His head toppled to the floor.

Padraig sprinted through the door. Pargiter had drunk the Aqua Monde water so he could fight off their prospective executioners. However, his self-sacrifice was over, the being in the lab was no longer the scientist. He was just as likely to attack them as the Navy Seals.
Anne and Flomo had tired of waiting for Padraig and they were already 30 yards ahead of him. The trio were racing through the science center heading for the water plant. The Seals may have destroyed all the boats in the dock but there was still one boat left on the island. The yacht Flomo and Anne had earlier stolen from Kevin Newman.

Padraig caught up with Anne and Flomo as they passed through the sliding glass doors into the water storage plant. The yacht was behind a further of doors just 50 feet across the sterile storage room. "We did it." Anne smiled at Flomo. They strolled calmly past the first row of water tanks. The danger had ceased, they were on their way home. Or so they thought. As they neared the second row of water tanks, a man stumbled out in front of them. It was Danny.

"Alright mate," said Padraig as he approached his friend. Danny was seemingly in pain, holding his left side and sighing. "No," said Anne as she grabbed Padraig's arm, "look at his face" Padraig peered more closely at his colleague. He looked very pale. His skin had a greyish complexion. His hand looked like an empty vinyl sack resting on fleshless bones. Danny let go of his midriff and clumsily stood up straight. His eyes were frosted over. His shirt was soaked with blood. "I guess I am going to have to put our friendship on ice," quipped Padraig darkly.

Danny stood between two rows of tankers occupying about a yard of space in an alley just six feet wide. The tanks extended to the roof and the walls. There was no other way around. They had to get past Danny if they were to escape the island. "Danny" cried a woman's voice from behind them. It was Edith. She was being followed by Gaunt, Mike and the rest of her group. She boldly strolled up alongside Padraig. Danny's mindless husk shimmied around as his empty eyes seemed to stare back. Padraig gripped Edith's hand. "It's not Danny. He's gone,"
"I know," said Edith.
"We have a boat," said Padraig "if we could get past him we can all get out of here."
"Then what are we waiting for?" asked Edith cheerfully. She approached Danny.
"What are you doing?" cried Padraig "Are you mad?"
"You know," said Edith "Danny and I had one thing in common. Neither of us have much of a life outside of here. He told me earlier, he sacrificed himself to save me, so that I could save others." Edith edged closer to Danny. She slipped her warm fingers between the cold dead appendages on his hands. "No it's my time to be the hero," she said sadly.
Edith pulled Danny towards her while leaning back to the water tank.

"Run," cried Flomo. "Come on" Billy Bradshaw ushered Sam and Ben through the gap Edith had created between Danny and the other water tank. The Patels followed, then Gaunt, Anne, and Flomo. Padraig stood motionless. He saw tears streaming down Edith's face. A thin trickle of blood rolled from the bottom of her skirt down the back of her leg. Edith's tears suddenly hardened midway down her throat. Her eyes rolled to the back of her head. Her sacrifice was complete. Padraig lingered for a moment. Pargiter, Danny, Edith; they had all sacrificed their own lives to save others. Was it worth it? Did he and these others deserve to be saved? Should it have been him that died and the others who lived? He brought Danny into this adventure. He manipulated Beauchamp to set in motion the events that cost the old man his life. It was Padraig who burst into Pargiter' laboratory and involved him in Anne's revenge schemes. Could it all have been avoided? Was it all worthwhile? As Edith's lifeless corpse slid free of Danny's icy grip, Padraig was sure of one thing. It was time to run.

Flomo made for the engine room with Anne following close behind. The surviving tourists collapsed onto deck chairs along the portside of the yacht. The engine began humming as the last passenger -- Padraig -- leaped from the dock onto the boat. "Stop right there," a familiar yet unwelcome voice emerged from the shadow of the water plant. It was Kevin Newman. "Who is he?" Gita asked Mike.
"I have no idea but he doesn't look friendly," responded her husband. Ben decided he could get a better view of the mysterious stranger if he climbed up the mast. It was slippery as the windy conditions had splatted the wooden pole with fresh sea water. He used the sail rings as makeshift stepping stones as he ascended the mast. "This my boat and I am taking it back," roared Newman. He was holding an assault rifle. All of the passengers were within easy range of the gun.
"We thought you were dead," yelled Padraig "we heard gunshots when you left with Furman."
"She is dead," Newman replied nonchalantly "they didn't see me. Now please get off my boat before I start firing this!"
"Why don't you just join us?" asked Gaunt.
"I need to be by myself," Kevin replied, "I need medical help."

His response unsettled Padraig. Newman had been in the lab when Pargiter explained the effects of the AM water on humans. Newman had also been in the hall where bottled water had been passed around to unwitting holidaymakers. "Did you drink the water, Kevin?" Padraig asked. Kevin clenched his left fist.
"I am perfectly fine. If you get out of my way I can get the medical attention I need."
"There is no medical attention," Padraig replied sympathetically "you know that Kevin. You're a scientist. These people here still have a chance. Don't take them down with you."

Newman paused for a moment and considered the group before him. A bombastic salesman, a troublesome journalist, some middle-aged strangers, and upon the deck -- his nemesis, Anne. He failed to notice young Billy who had made his way halfway up the mast. The boy's sneakers were worn after months of playing soccer on hardcourts. His grip on the mast ring was about to slip.

Newman shook his head. "I gave you a chance, but you leave me no alternative." Newman aimed his rifle at the Bradshaws and began to squeeze the trigger. The ragged sole of Ben's left sneaker suddenly gave way and the youngster plunged from the mast towards the deck. His fall was broken as he hit the boom -- the wooden pole running on the underside of the sail. The impact of the 80-pound child on the timber, caused the boom to spin violently in a full circle. Padraig ducked as the wood brushed over his head. It continued its rotation as it swept over the edge of the dock. Seeing an opportunity for further heroism, Billy jumped up and grabbed the back side of the boom. With all his weight he helped to increase its momentum as it collided with Newman's shins. The impact caused the scientist to tumble into the ocean below. A series of large bubbles burst from the site of Kevin's descent into the sea. A single, grey looking, icy hand broke the surface for a second, before the contaminated scientist slipped into the depths of the ocean.

The passengers were silent as the yacht sped away from Aqua Monde. Flomo was at the helm. Gaunt had conceded defeat in trying to operate the vessel. Mike and Gita sat on deck watching the island fade into the distance as the sun set. As it neared the horizon, two silent missiles descended from above and gently glided to the island. They were too far out to hear the sound or even to feel the waves vibrate. But the spectacular explosion illuminated the dusk sky. The island was gone forever. The Americans had taken the Soviet option. Conceal what you cannot control.

Two Days Later,

It was a chilly winter's morning in Uruguay. Playa Brava's one sandy shoreline was deserted, save for a few pensioners scouring the shoreline for seashells. One incongruous object was scruffing up the shoreline. It was a large yacht. Garishly painted with a logo that read 'Aqua Monde' which translates as Waterworld. A group of weary-looking travelers were descending from the boat down a ladder. They formed a single-file line across the beach as they headed for firmer land. An African man led the way, his arm around a fair-haired girl. A scruffy looking journalist trailed in their wake. One of his countrymen followed in his shadow with his family close behind. At the rear was an Indian woman who walked a few steps ahead of her husband. He walked side by side with a very animated man.

"You know Mike, I have to say you have had the whole sales pitch," joked Gaunt.
"I mean some clients you wine and dine, but hey buddy we have escaped exploding islands together, dodged bullets and hostile ice men. We have been through a hell of a lot. I was wondering at what point, does a guy earn your trust? Can I call you a client yet Mike? Will you invest with me?" Mike stopped walking and turned to face Gaunt. He pursed his lips while he contemplated his response. Gaunt stood wide-eyed in anticipation of his response like a dog begging for a treat.
"You know Mr. Gaunt" Mike said, "I would very much like to be your client."
Gaunt smiled cheerfully, winked and extended a firm hand. Patel reciprocated, grasping Gaunt's hand tightly. As he did so, Gaunt became aware that Patel's hand was unusually cold. Ice cold.

Printed in Great Britain
by Amazon